To: Heather
thank you!

Michelle Johnson

This is a work of fiction. Names, characters, places and incidents are products of the author's imagination or are used fictitiously and are not to be constructed as real. Any resemblance to actual events, persons, living or dead, is entirely coincidental.

First Printing: 2015

ISBN#: 978-1-329-26727-5

All inquiries can be made on the contact page found on website below.

www.oleahchronicles.com

Book cover designed by Michelle Johnson

Oleah Chronicles
TRUTH

MICHELLE JOHNSON

Acknowledgements

I would like to thank my editors, Vanessa, Ann-Marie and Lauren without whose help this book would never have been completed. Your suggestions, critiques and encouragement helped mold this book into what it is today.

Lauren: For your willingness to help with all badgering emails, texts and moments of doubt. Thank you.

Ann and Vanessa: Proper sentence structure. Who knew such a thing existed? (wink wink) Thank you for your guidance. Finally, to Vanessa again, for allowing me to use that gorgeous face as the billboard and brand of this series.

This book is dedicated to Alana, Alicia, Lauryn, Natalie, Peyton and Vanessa.
No dream is ever too small to reach for.

INTRO

"Quick, this way!" The tribal soldier yelled back over the sounding alarms. "We must hurry, Coral can only hold the portal open for a few minutes. It's our only chance to escape the Dark Seekers."

"Where will we go?" The tribal queen yelled as she hurried to gather the rest of her belongings. "How do you know it's safe?" The panic was thick in her voice as she tied a knot over the opening to her bag and threw it over her shoulder. Her cappuccino colored skin blanched with anxiety.

The soldier quickly grabbed her hand and began to run, leading the way. "Coral will explain everything, my queen, the king is already there waiting with the princess." He hastily led her through the back door of the palace that opened out to the path that would bring them into the jungle.

It was sunset, the sky burned with deep oranges and fiery reds. Loud crashes and earth-shaking thuds boomed in the background. The crackling of the fires roared and screams of panic echoed. It was chaos.

The planet Uforika was under attack from the sorceress, accompanied by thousands of creatures from Kindren, the Land of Darkness, to destroy one thing, and one thing only: the princess.
As the two flew out into the jungle, they transformed into white lions, sprinting through the lush forestation without a second to spare.

"This way!" the lion instructed, and he directed them right on the fork in the path that led to a waterfall behind which they speedily entered a small opening into a secret tunnel. As soon as they were safely inside, they transformed back into their Oleah form.

An Oleah could be described as a creature with a combination of human and lion features. The top half of their faces resembled that of a lion, the bottom half human, along with a human torso and lion legs from the waist down. They were among the most powerful mystical creatures throughout the galaxies.

Through the darkness, the queen could make out a green light ahead. As they came around the bend, they found the tribal Oleah king holding the two-year-old princess in his arms. Beside him was a cherub named Coral with flowing strawberry blond curls that ran down her back over her blue satin robe. An oval-shaped Portal that glowed light green, danced wildly in circles behind them. Once Coral and the tribal king saw the queen and the soldier, a look of relief swept over both of their faces. Coral's pearl white wings spread out from behind her back and fluttered with excitement as she glided in the air.

"My queen." She smiled brightly, revealing her angelic dimples.

"You made it, thank the heavens!" The tribal king sighed and ran over to embrace the queen. The little princess giggled as she reached out from in between her parents to grab her mother's shell necklace with excitement.

The queen smiled, looking down with adoration at her daughter, cupping her face gently as tears welled in her tawny eyes. "My little cub. Mama's here now."

The soldier grinned, pleased that he was able to successfully reunite the family, his tanned complexion flushed from the run. He gave a nod of greeting to Coral. She slightly smiled, returning the nod and promptly glided back to the ground in front of the portal.

She cleared her throat and began with urgency in her voice:
"There's not much time, the portal will close in five minutes."

The king and queen anxiously acknowledged Coral's statement with a nod and turned back to the soldier for their final goodbyes. The king pressed his forehead against the soldier's as they firmly placed their right hands on the back of each other's necks. The king's voice was firm, but pained.

"Kovu, you have been loyal to me and my family, and for that I shall not forget you."

The princess giggled as she reached up for Kovu. "Ko-Ko!"

Kovu forced a smile despite his sadness and leaned down to press his forehead onto the princess'. He cleared his throat to try and dispel the lump that sat heavily in it.

"Little Princess Angel, I will miss you. May the strength of the lioness within protect you, little cub."

Princess Angel's bright lion-like eyes looked back at him with a mixture of confusion and playfulness. Kovu bowed his head to remove one of his many necklaces filled with lion claws and feathers, and placed it delicately around the princess' neck.

Moved by Kovu's gift, the king held back tears as a grin lifted the corners of his lips, and walked back over to stand next to Coral with the little princess in his arms. The queen then approached Kovu, embracing him in the same way.

"Protect what's left of our people. *You* will be their leader until it is safe for us to return so Angel can fulfill her destiny. Give them hope, be kind but firm, and assure them that we will live in peace again."

The queen let go of Kovu and gave him one last look. Her face warm, but her tawny eyes were anguished as the portal glowed against her cappuccino skin and long black curly hair.

Kovu tried to give a reassuring grin. "Your legacy will live on in our new Kingdom, that I promise you ..." His voice broke, emotions too thick to continue. He gestured towards the portal. "You must go, my queen."

The queen briskly walked with a heavy heart over to stand with her family. Coral looked up at them and spoke clearly but quickly.

"This portal leads to the planet Earth. You will become human, and lose all powers on this planet, but you will be safe. We've gotten everything set up there so that you can enter their world unnoticed and live among them without suspicion. You will not be able to contact our world, however I will have the power to speak to you and update you through signs in the stars. Look for them when the moon is full. *Only* then will you regain the power to hear my thoughts. If danger from Kindren is near, you will be able to access your powers, but in small doses. It's best if the princess has no knowledge of our world, and lives her life as a regular human. From what I know, I am the only cherub with access to this portal. The Sorceress has not figured out the formula to replicate a cherub's wing glitter, and hopefully it will stay that way." She flapped her wings and glided swiftly into the air above the portal. "Now hurry, once you're through the portal my wing glitter will close it behind you. Peace be with you."

The king bowed his head in appreciation to Coral, gave a final glance back at Kovu and went through the portal with Princess Angel smiling and waving, "BYE-BYE!"

The queen hesitated, looking up to Coral. "What if Angel is found? I won't have my full power to protect her?"

Coral looked warily at the queen with her childlike features. "My queen, you will regain your full powers *only if* the Sorceress takes a portal to Earth. Let us pray to the heavens that it does not come to that. I give you my word, I will protect Princess Angel." Her words were full of conviction, filling the tribal queen with a peace that tingled throughout her body.

The queen smiled softly for the last time at Coral. "Peace be with you." She took in a deep breath, and walked through the portal.

Chapter 1: Hello Stranger

BEEP! BEEP! BEEP! BEEP! *SMACK!*

"OK, OK, I'm up." I mumbled, my voice still groggy from sleep, and plopped myself back on my pillow. I absolutely hated early mornings, particularly Monday mornings. Having to leave the warmth of my cozy bed to get up for school after weekends of sleeping in, and staying up late, was always brutal.

There was a sudden rap on the door.

"Angel, are you up, sweetie?" dad's voice whispered loudly from behind my door.

"Ummhmm."

I forced myself to sit up, my legs dangling over the edge of the bed. "Just about to get in the shower."

"Ok, well get a move on, you don't want to be late for your test this morning," he stressed before making his way down the hall.

"Yeah, yeah, yeah."

I got up and staggered sleepily towards my door to grab my towel that hung on the back. Test days were always the same. Dad would come knocking on the door to make sure I actually woke up, then tell Mom to get a bowl of cereal ready for me downstairs before bombarding me with a bunch of test questions to make sure I was actually ready. All that because of that *one* time I overslept and bombed my test. They'll never let me live it down. I got to school late and only had a half hour to finish the test that I was *totally* not prepared for, which resulted in a big fat F. I was forbidden to watch TV for a week after that fiasco. Mom claimed that if I hadn't stayed up watching TV the night before, I would have had more time to study and I would have passed the test. Whatever. My teacher has had it out for me since day one, so studying wouldn't have made much of a difference anyway.

I walked down the hall into the bright sun-filled bathroom and looked out the window. It was going to be a decent cloudless, sunny day in Toronto. It was mid-May, so the weather was still bipolar, teasing us with warm sunny days before reverting back to cold, grey wet ones. I stood at the window letting the sun warm my face before I hung up my towel and got the water going. With an oversized yawn, I looked into the mirror, wiping the sleep out of my eyes.

I looked a mess. My thick but smooth curly black hair was a hairball of fly-aways in a messy bun. My eyes, still puffy from sleep, looked even more dramatic against my light cappuccino-toned skin.

My whole family, that being Mom, Dad and me, had hazel and gold colored eyes. They were very cat-like. I've had so many people come up to me at school to tell me how cool my eyes are because of how much they resembled a lion's. Mom says it's because we're descendants of the Leeu Tribe. The legend was that the Leeu tribe actually became lions, and were great fighters and protectors of their people. I've never seen anyone else with our particular eye color, so it makes my family kind of unique. That being said, it also makes me feel like a freak show. I hated the attention and would much rather blend in like everyone else. It's stressful enough being sixteen. I've made peace with my curvy medium build, but still had a lot of work to do in the confidence department. In no way did I dislike myself, I just found it very difficult at times to communicate in crowds. The whole social party scene was one that I avoided like the plague.

"Angel, you've got twenty minutes!" Mom yelled from downstairs. I grumbled and got in the shower.

After my shower, I quickly brushed my teeth, got dressed and pulled my damp curly hair into a high ponytail. Once I determined I was decent enough, I went downstairs into the kitchen and took a seat at the table in front of my huge bowl of Golden Grahams. I scooped up a large mouthful while Mom stood on the other side of the counter pouring herself a cup of coffee. Her long, curly black hair highlighted with sandy blonde streaks, pulled back with a white headband to keep it out of her face. She loved to braid little strands of her hair and put little shells at the bottom. She said it made her feel like she was back in the village where she grew up off the coast of Africa.

Mom always talked about how great her village used to be. It's where she met and married my dad before riots forced them to become refugees. They came to Canada when I was two to give me a better life. I don't remember anything about the place, I guess I was too young, and I don't even know any of my other family; it's always just been the three of us. She, wore brown dress pants, with a white-collared buttoned up shirt and a brown-and-blue checkered vest. She always looked so professional and powerful, not to mention that she was drop dead gorgeous. She looked like Halle Berry, except more exotic, almost like an Amazonian warrior. I always hear from neighbors and friends of my parents, how much I resemble my mother. As flattered as I was by their compliments, I was convinced that I would never be as pretty as her. Our skin tones were very similar, except I had more of my dad's lighter complexion while Mom was more of a caramel tone.

As she stirred cream and sugar into her coffee, she turned to me with her classic you-better-know-the-answers-to-these-questions look. She took a quick sip of her coffee before the interrogation began.

"Did you have a chance to review last night for your English test today?"

"Yup," I said around a mouthful of cereal. *Here we go*, I thought.

"Good. So, what was the name of Juliet's cousin whom Romeo murdered?"

"Tybalt."

She raised an eyebrow skeptically. "Who was Mercutio?"

"Easy. Romeo's best friend. C'mon Mom, you gotta do better than that." I teased, taking another bite of cereal.

She smiled mischievously at me and said, "Where did Juliet get the idea to fake her death?"

"The Priest."

With another sip of coffee, she folded her arms in a calculating manner.

"Did I pass?"

"Let's hope so." She failed attempting to hide her grin.

I picked up a soggy square out of the bowl and flicked it at her. It successfully met its target, landing on the hand she held her coffee mug with. I burst into laughter as she shook her head with strong disapproval, slowly peeling off the soggy square.

"Very funny. C'mon, finish up, we're leaving in three minutes."

She fluidly took one last sip of coffee, placed the cup in the sink, grabbed the keys that hung off the wall and headed for the front door.

"Honey, don't forget to pick up some steaks for dinner tonight!" she yelled up the stairs.

After my last gigantic mouthful, I quickly placed my bowl in the sink and grabbed my backpack off the stairs before yelling goodbye to Dad and walking out the door.

My dad is lucky; he got to go back to bed after his usual wake-up duties. He was an artist who had his own gallery, so he pretty much makes his own hours. His art was really cool. He specialized in wildlife canvases, particularly lions. They were his favorite. He painted this amazing picture that hung in their bedroom of two white lions and their cub. The detail that he put into each painting was incredible.

As we pulled up in front of the school, per usual, Julie, my best friend, was waiting for me on the steps. She always asked to get dropped off early, knowing that two minutes later I'd be there. She was wearing her favorite dark red sweater that perfectly complemented her alabaster skin, piercing ocean blue eyes and wavy jet black hair. She greeted me with a smile before beginning to make faces through the window. She always cracked me up. If you wanted a good laugh, especially when you felt crappy, Julie was the person to see.

"Hey Mrs. Seriki," she beamed as I got out of the car.

"Good morning, Julie, all prepared for the test I assume?"

Because I've known Julie since kindergarten, she's become an honorary member of the family, which basically means she gets the same lectures I do. Julie rolled her eyes and nudged me with her elbow. I snorted a laugh, as she gave Mom her monotone response.

"Yes, Mrs. Seriki."

"That's what I like to hear." Mom leaned over the seat. "OK, girls, see you after school, and Angel, remember 3:30pm *sharp*, there's no reason you girls can't socialize in the car on the way home."

In unison, Julie and I both rolled our eyes as I answered.

"Yeah, I know, Mom."

Mom was such a drill sergeant when it came to these things. If I didn't call her when I was going over to Julie's place after school the moment I got there, she'd hunt me down. I remember this one time I forgot to call her because Julie and I were freaking out over the fact that Robert (the hottest guy in school) accidentally bumped into us, grabbed my shoulder and said, *"Oops!* Sorry, hon." We were dying all the way home, jumping, giggling and planning my future wedding. Anyone would have gotten sidetracked over that! Mom ended up showing up at Julie's house with the look of death on her face: she was *not* a happy camper at all.

Speaking of hot guys, the whole boyfriend department is non-existent. I'm not allowed to date *period*. If a guy were interested in me - which no one in my school has yet made vocal - I imagine Mom would interrogate him so bad that he would most likely not be interested in me anymore. She was super protective, that's pretty much the bottom line. It was really annoying, Dad wasn't nearly as bad, but sometimes I could see him trying to restrain from asking a hundred and one questions about my whereabouts.

"OK, good luck, ladies." Mom blew a kiss and waved as she drove away.

As soon as she turned the corner, officially out of sight, Julie turned to me excitedly. "OK, we have a party to plan."

Julie wanted this big huge party for my seventeenth birthday two weeks from now, marking the end of school and the beginning of summer vacation. I, on the other hand, just wanted to do something small like cook up a few burgers and have a bonfire in the backyard.

"Jewls, I don't want to have a party."

She crossed her arms in obvious annoyance. "Listen, Angel, whether you like it or not, to your family seventeen is party material."

According to my parents, turning seventeen back in their village meant the beginning of adulthood.

"Why can't we just chill out, have some burgers and relax around a fire? You know my dad tells the best stories."

"Ya, I know, but you can still do all of that with like, fifty people."

I felt my eyes bug. "*Fifty* people! Are you crazy? I don't even *know* fifty people." Julie's face fell. "Look," I continued, trying to placate her, "I know you want to make it special, but to me it will only be special if I'm surrounded by the people I care about the most. Not just people who want to come and eat all our food."

She smiled a little. "And who would those special people be?"

"*Duh*, Mom, Dad and me."

"Angel!" She whined, slapping my arm.

I couldn't help but laugh, she was so gullible. "I'm kidding!"

Julie crossed her arms.

"Oh, come on, how could I *not* have you there, Jewls, be serious."

She smiled. "I know, I'm the life of the party!" She looked at her watch, then back up at me in a panic. "It's 8:15! We have five minutes to get inside before the bell goes."

We both ran inside to our lockers, which were of course, side by side. As I opened my locker door, a cold chill swept over me; my skin prickled with goose bumps. I shivered as I rubbed my hand over my arms to try and dispel the lingering icy sensation. *Strange*, I thought. There are no doors leading outside anywhere near my locker, plus we were too far from the main entrance to feel wind. I moved the door just enough to look at Julie.

"Geez, did you feel that?"

She was barely listening to me in her rush to take off her backpack and grab her books.

"Feel what?"

"The negative-forty-degree breeze that just came by. It was *freezing*, how could you not have felt that?"

She paused, held her books in one hand, tucked her backpack under her chin and put her free hand on my forehead. "Maybe you're getting sick." She put her hand back down. "You feel fine to me."

She shrugged her shoulders, and went back to her crazy frenzy of trying to get organized.

I chuckled at her state of disorganization, as I hung up my jacket, grabbed my books from my bag and closed the locker. When I turned around, I felt the cold breeze again, but this time it seemed to circle around me. I shivered and was about to say to Julie that she must be feeling it now, but something else had caught my attention. I sensed someone was watching me and it was enough to make me uncomfortable. I turned my head right to look down the hallway. Nothing. I turned the other direction and there was a guy leaning on the corner of the wall down the hall with his hands crossed against his chest staring right at me.

When our eyes met, I found myself locked in his stare, a slow grin began forming on his full lips. The hallway was packed, yet it felt like it was just the two of us standing there. It was as if he'd come straight out of a magazine: he was very tall, at least six feet with chiselled features, dark brown hair that fell to his temples, and dressed in all black. His creamy ivory skin was flawless, not to mention the perfect dimples in his cheeks. There was no doubt about it; he was gorgeous.

"Oh. My. God." I said. Julie, who had gotten everything she needed out of her locker, looked at me with curiosity as she shut the door.

"What?"

"Extreme hottie alert," I said, trying to speak out of the corner of my mouth without breaking my gaze with him. He continued to stare, his grin widening.

"Oh my gosh, where?" Julie asked in giddy excitement.

The bell rang and the hallways were suddenly flooded with people on their way to class. I tried to keep my eyes on him, but too many people were in the way. Julie gasped, grabbed my arm and started to pull me through the crowd to get to our class. I threw one last look over my shoulder, but he was gone.

We ran into class just before Ms. Foster closed the door. She gave us a very unimpressed look as we walked past her and took our seats.

"OK, class, you have sixty minutes to write the test. Those who finish early can start taking notes from page 355 in their textbook. When I hand out the papers, keep them face-down until I tell you to begin. Please no talking."

Julie looked over at me and mouthed the words: *Who was it? Robert?*

Checking to make sure Ms. Foster wasn't looking, I leaned over to whisper back, "No, I've never seen him before."

Julie smiled, rubbing her hands together and mouthed: *Fresh meat!*

We both giggled softly.

Ms. Foster came down our aisle to hand out the test papers, clearing her throat loudly as she approached us and slapped the papers on our desks.

"I said *no talking.*"

We instantly turned to face the front of the room. Once she finished the row, she turned to face everyone.

"Begin."

As I flipped through the papers to read over the questions, I smiled smugly to myself. I had this test in the bag, I knew the answer to every question. Mom would be so proud. I whipped through the answers, finishing before anyone else in the class. Once I handed in my test, I started going through the textbook to start on the boring notes.

I glanced out the small window in the door and had to do a double take. There was the Extreme Hottie walking past the door! As he walked by, he slowed to look right at me, giving me the most breathtaking smile. I felt my face go red and looked down, biting back my smile. When I looked back up again he was gone. Who *was* this guy? He had to be new, I've never seen him around before. I tried to digest what just happened in my head and couldn't get over his smile. The thought of the new hottest guy in school being interested in me had me grinning like a fool.

"Psst!" Julie whispered, resting her head in her arms. I hadn't even noticed she finished her test. "I *so* passed that test."

I hunched over, trying to hide behind my textbook. "Me too, I knew every answer!"

Ms. Foster scolded us from her desk. "Ladies, the test is still in session, be respectful to the other students. I had asked that you take notes on page 355, so I strongly suggest you stop the chatter and get to it."

I grumbled and went back to the notes. Once class was dismissed, Julie linked arms with me.

"Geez, she *so* hates us."

We both giggled and went back to our lockers for our second period class. She had science, while I had history, so we arranged to meet back up for lunch.

History, as usual, was the class that I could easily catch up on some Z's without the teacher noticing. Today was movie day. We got to watch documentaries on World War II, meaning I had the whole class to take a nap.

We got let out early once the movie finished, giving me an extra ten minutes until Julie got out of class. I put my books inside my locker, and sat down, leaning my back against the door and took out my phone to play Tetris. I was on level 5 when an icy chill swept over me. I heard footsteps coming down the empty hall. I glanced up to see the principal, Mr. Frank, walking with the Extreme Hottie, giving him a tour. I felt my stomach flip as I tried to play it cool.

"So this is our language hall, where we have our Spanish, Latin and French classes. I'm sure you will find that our methods of teaching are up to the standards you are accustomed to coming from Eastern Mills." Mr. Frank held up his head proudly.

The Extreme Hottie grinned and responded, "Yes, I'm sure they are. I look forward to putting that to the test." His voice was low and raspy, but smooth. He sounded so sophisticated.

Eastern Mills High School was in New York City, a school for gifted kids. So he was not only drop-dead gorgeous, but extremely smart too. I tried to appear indifferent with my head bent over my phone as they passed by. A cold shiver ran down my spine again. I looked up once their backs were to me and in that moment, he glanced over at me with a smirk before turning back to continue on his tour. My heart jumped into my throat.

"How was your nap?"

Startled, I looked up to see Julie.

She snorted. "Having an out-of-earth experience I see. What has you so spaced out?"

I instantly stood in excitement. "Remember the Extreme Hottie I was telling you about?"

Her eyes gleamed with excitement. "What about him?"

"OK, I know this sounds stupid, but I swear he's either into me or making fun of me, I don't know. This morning when I first noticed him, he was staring at me."

Julie cried out in giddy excitement. "It's love at first sight!"

I teasingly slapped her arm. "Get this, in English this morning, after I finished my test, he was walking by, saw me in the class and gave me the biggest smile. Then, just now, Mr. Frank was giving him a tour, so he's obviously new to the school, and when they passed by, he practically broke his neck to smile at me again."

Julie started jumping up and down. "No way!" She stopped jumping, closed her eyes and tried to collect herself. "OK, breathe, Angel. First things first, I need to see this guy. If he's going to be your future boyfriend, he needs my approval."

"He's *not* going to be my future boyfriend because one: he looks like he's a senior. Two: he's a genius, so he'll eventually see that there are other far more hot and intelligent girls in this school, and three –" I paused, trying to think of how to say what I was thinking in a way that didn't make me look stupid.

"C'mon, spit it out!" Julie shook my shoulders.

I hesitated for a second. "This is nuts, but I swear to you, every time he walks by, I get this chill."

"Ok, Angel, he *totally* likes you! You just feel a little taken aback because you're not used to guys around here showing that much attention to anything other than themselves. It's natural that you have the chills because it's new to you. And who cares if he is a senior, you'll be seventeen in two weeks, so technically, worst case scenario, he's a year older, year and a half tops."

I sighed. "I guess."

Julie put one hand on her hip, raising an eyebrow. "How are you so sure he's a genius?"

Chuckling, I responded, "I heard Mr. Frank say he's from Eastern Mills."

Julie's eyes widened. "THE Eastern Mills?"

I nodded.

"He *is* a genius! So why is he coming here?" she demanded. "Shouldn't he be going to some other gifted school?"

"Who knows, Jewls, but I'm starving. Let's get something to eat."

She put her books in her locker and we made our way to the cafeteria. Julie got pizza, I went for fries and gravy. Not the most nutritional food, but definitely the most cost-effective.

Throughout lunch, Julie babbled on about how much she hates her science class and all the potential ways that she can make a love connection between me and Mr. Extreme Hottie. I found myself daydreaming, replaying the encounters with him in my head.

Lunch went by in a flash and I was back at my locker getting ready for the next class. Julie was lucky. She had a spare, so she got an extra-long lunch. I, on the other hand, had to sit through career studies. I guess that's what I get for trying to fast-track and graduate sooner. I missed out on all the spares.

It felt like an eternity for career studies to be over. The teacher Mrs. Hadwick gave the most boring lecture about finding the right job to suit your personality and how she had to spend two years in self-discovery so that she could find the right job for her and blah, blah, blah.
Once the bell rang, I bolted out of there so fast. I needed some stimulation for my brain, and looked forward to seeing Julie in Spanish. Time always went by so much faster when we were in class together. When I got to class, Julie had already saved me the empty spot beside her.

I plopped down in my seat with an exasperated sigh. "Career studies was *brutal*. What did you do?"

She grinned mischievously. "I went on a hunt for the Extreme Hottie."

"How? You don't even know what he looks like."

She shook her head, dismissing me. "Well, obviously he's going to be the only hot guy in the school that I haven't seen before."

"OK, true. So, how did you make out?"

She deflated in disappointment. "Nothing."

I chuckled at the thought of Julie trying to be a spy. She would give away her cover by becoming giddy to the point of snorting if she had actually found him.

As the last batch of students settled in their seats, Mr. Frank came in followed by the Extreme Hottie. Mrs. Jonahs, our Spanish teacher, rose from her seat in delight.

"Ah, this must be Zander!"

Mr. Frank nodded pleasantly to Mrs. Jonahs and turned to address the class.

"Everyone, this is Zander Black. He's our newest student here at Willowing Peaks."

Mr. Frank was never so formal when introducing a new student; you could tell he was going out of his way to make an impression.

Julie gasped, her mouth wide open. She quickly turned, mouthing to me: *That's him?* I nodded to her in disbelief. How could he be in *this* class? It was a junior class.

Mr. Frank patted Zander on the shoulders. "Mrs. Jonahs was a professor in Chile, and she has an exquisite knowledge of Spanish culture and art. I'm sure you'll learn many new exciting things."

Mrs. Jonahs smiled confidently. "Thank you, Mr. Frank. From what I've heard, Zander, I just might learn new things from you too." She gestured to the class. "Please take a seat, there's one right there." She pointed to the seat directly beside me, and my heart took a flying leap. He locked eyes with me and said to her without looking back, "Excellent, thank you."

Mr. Frank left, and Mrs. Jonahs started to write the class outline on the chalkboard. My heart was beating so fast I thought the whole room could hear it. Zander took his seat beside me. Already I could feel the weight of his stares. I slowly turned my head, and with a slow, sly smile, he addressed me.

"Hello stranger."

Chapter 2: The Night Speaks

Mouth dry, I responded in a voice barely louder than a whisper. "*Hi.*"

I awkwardly turned back to face the front of the class, suddenly feeling very insecure. I was frozen in place, trying hard to focus on the chalkboard when I heard him say,

"What's your name?"

All logical thinking had officially left my brain. "Uhhh …"

Julie, who had been watching every second, nudged me to snap out of it. It didn't work. I continued to stare like a deer caught in headlights at Zander. He stared back expectantly, his smile growing wider as the seconds went by. Let the freak show, that is my life, begin. I would be sure to have a good cry about this mortifying moment later.

Julie nudged me again, whispering under her breath, "Angel, are you *serious* right now?"

"Angel. That's a lovely name." His low raspy voice whispered back to me.

Utterly humiliated, I glared at Julie. She threw her hands up in surrender, shaking her head at me, mouthing, Not my fault. I turned back to him with an awkward smile, finally finding my voice. "Thank you."

"Your eyes are…very striking."

I felt my face begin to burn with heat. I must have looked like a bright red tomato. Finally seeing him up close, I realized his eyes were just as strange as mine. They were an auburn color with almost more red than brown. The contrast of his eyes against his creamy skin made his chiselled features stand out even more. I tried my best to stop staring, feeling the cotton balls in my mouth slowly diminish as I managed to respond.

"Yeah, thanks. I, uh, get that a lot."

I couldn't keep eye contact with him for too long, the magnitude of his stare was almost intimidating.

"I'm Julie, Angel's best friend," Julie jumped in. "So, what brings you to Toronto?"

Julie was overly perky, more so than usual. I bit down a smile, grateful that at least we could both look like fools together.

"My family and I moved here a couple weeks ago. My parents are scientists, their job moved us here for special research on a new project." As he said the last part, his eyes met mine.

"Cool," Julie could barely stay in her seat; she was leaning so far over her desk just to be in the conversation. "What's the project?"

"Well, if I told you …" The corner of his lips pulled up in a smug smile. "I'd have to kill you."

Julie burst into high-pitched laughter. I closed my eyes, shamefaced at how we must look to him.

"OK! Everyone settle down," Mrs. Jonahs said loudly. "On the board I have written down several sentences in Spanish with errors in them. Your task is to tell me what is wrong with the sentence. Let's begin with the first line. Who would like to go first? Zander, how about you?"

He broke his gaze on us and looked to the front board. He repeated the sentence in Spanish with a fluent accent. "The sentence begins with 'yo', then proceeds with 'mi'. It doesn't make sense to say 'I, myself', it should just be 'yo' at the beginning."

Mrs. Jonahs beamed, "Very good, Zander, your Spanish is exceptional!"

"Thank you. At my previous school, Spanish was one of my favourite subjects."

"Wonderful! Alright, next sentence? Myra?"

The class continued on with the other students trying to answer the questions and Mrs. Jonahs asking Zander if he knew the right answers and why. Julie gave me little nudges throughout the class whispering things like "I approve" and "He definitely likes you!" I rolled my eyes at her, feeling more and more self-conscious at how embarrassingly awkward I was with him. He was definitely very smart, and surprisingly polite and charismatic, which unfortunately brought his level of perfection up several notches, thus making him that much more intimidating to me. At the end of class, he got up to get his things together, and glanced over.

"Angel. Julie. It was nice meeting you two. I hope we can see more of each other. I don't know a lot of people around here. Maybe you girls can show me around?"

"Oh my gosh, of *course!*" Julie beamed.

I nodded, giving another awkward smile in his direction. He smiled back and headed for the door, turning just before leaving to wink at me.

"We have to get you two together!" Julie erupted.

I found myself irrationally annoyed by her constant match-maker bit. "Jewls, are you kidding? You saw how much of a freak I am with him, there's no chance in hell that's happening."

"But he likes you! And he's our age!"

I snapped. "Who cares? Just because you think something is a good idea doesn't mean I have to agree. Back off, will you!"

I instantly regretted those words. I hated snapping at Julie, she was so sensitive. The hurt in her eyes spread across her face. I knew the damage was done and the retaliation would soon follow.

Her eyes narrowed into slits. "Just a little re-cap, Angel: *you* were the one who made such a big deal about him all day, so excuse me if I get excited because I care." She grabbed her books and stomped out of the classroom.

I let out a breath in frustration, picked up the rest of my books and headed towards our lockers. Julie was now giving me the silent treatment. She waited with her backpack on and arms tightly crossed. I grabbed my backpack and locked my locker.

"Jewls, I'm sorry, OK. I guess I'm just a little overwhelmed."

She didn't answer. I stood staring, trying to persuade her to talk to me. On the third attempt, I glanced down at my watch. 3:29pm.

"We have one minute to get to my mom's car before she lectures us all the way home, so I suggest we start walking."

With one swift movement, she turned on her heels and started walking ahead of me. Sure enough, Mom was waiting in the parking lot. Julie got in the back with her arms still crossed.

"Hey ladies, how was the test?" Mom asked with a cheery smile.

We both sat in our seats straight-faced. "Fine." I answered very monotone.

Mom gave me a curious look, turned around to check out Julie, then turned back to face the front. "Huh. Bad day, ladies?"

"Mom, can we just go?"

"So ... anyone want to tell me why the both of you have come into my car with your negative energy?" Mom asked as she put the car in drive.

Silence.

"Angel?" Mom pressed.

"*She's* the one not talking to me, I apologized already and she still refuses to talk, so if anyone has brought in bad energy, it's her." I couldn't help but get a little upset about it even though I was in the wrong for snapping at her. She was just being difficult.

Julie jumped in. "UGH! You brought this upon *yourself*, your apology was *so* not genuine."

"Yes it was! I said sorry like three times, what do you want me to do? Beg? Come *on*, Jewls, be serious."

"Girls –" Mom tried.

"I *am* being serious! You totally blew up at me for no good reason. It's not that big a deal."

"Girls –"

"Yes it is! You can't just go and try and make decisions for me, Julie."

"I wasn't! Zander is the one who has made it obvious that he likes you, not me."

"GIRLS!"

We both fell silent. We knew that tone all too well.

"Listen to the both of you, it's shameful," Mom hissed, shaking her head from side to side. "Who's Zander? Don't tell me you guys are fighting over a boy."

I turned to glare at Julie. "Thanks a lot."

"I asked you a question, Angel."

I groaned, rolling my eyes. "He's this new kid at school."

"I need to meet this boy."

"Mom, NO!"

Julie chuckled. "Mrs. Seriki, I can assure you, Angel is not interested. She made *that* quite clear."

Mom smiled contentedly. "Good. Teenage boys just bring trouble with them."

"Mom! Can we *not* talk about this?"

Mom continued to smile, zipping her mouth with one hand. "So, am I taking you home then, Julie?"

Julie continued to stare out the window, straight-faced. "Yup."

The rest of the ride home was silent. After dropping Julie off, I went straight to my room to lie down. I felt exhausted. I never liked fighting, especially with Julie, so when I did, it definitely took a toll on me. There was a soft knock on my door.

"Sweetie? Are you going to come down for dinner? The steaks are mean and lean," Dad said softly from the other side of the door.

"I'm not very hungry, Dad, can you guys leave me a plate?"

He opened the door to peek his head inside. "Everything alright, Angel? Your mom told me you had a fight with Julie." His forehead wrinkled in concern. "Want to talk about it?"

"Not really, but thanks, Dad. I just want to be left alone and relax."

He nodded, giving me a gentle smile. "I know just the trick."

He left my room, and within a minute he was back with pink incense in his hands. He set them down on my table, lighting the ends. "It's Maolita, from the village where your mother and I were born. The scent is great for a nice calm, renewing wellness and good feelings. Just let yourself drift with it and you'll feel great afterward." He leaned forward and kissed my forehead.

"Thanks, Dad."

My parents were naturalists. They always had some candle or incense burning. Dad always reminisced with stories of the exotic smells from their village and how you could smell them from a mile away and feel safe. He said no feeling compared to returning back to the village after a hunt, when the energy was high and the scents welcomed them home with their familiarity.

I took a few deep breaths in and exhaled. I found myself drifting away, allowing my new state of calm to take the tension out of my body as I became more relaxed. I tried to fight sleep, but eventually it took me under.

* * * * *

I heard the sound of birds chirping, and felt the heat of a warm sun beating down on me. Fresh scents of vanilla and coconut filled the air. I opened my eyes.

I was facing a beautiful lush jungle from a balcony railing. I looked down to see there were a pack of lions pacing back and forth. I should have been scared to death, but instead I looked at them and smiled, feeling very secure. I turned around to face the room behind me. It was a gorgeous bedroom laced with dark wood. The bed had four high pillars that were entangled with white lace fabric. The sheets were tan mixed with whites and greens, atop which sat large fluffy pillows. There were hibiscus flowers surrounding the room with pink incenses burning. The walls had intricate paintings with symbols and twirling designs in gold. I felt like I was in a castle.

"Whoa!"

I walked through the room to the double doors opposite, opened them and peered out. The hallways were lit with candles hanging from the walls and huge green leaves taken right out of the jungle. I slowly started walking down the hall and came to a winding staircase that led to the front door. When I reached the door, I heard voices coming from the other side. I put my ear against it to try and listen but the words were too muffled to understand. I pulled on the door handles to open them and a cold breeze hit me.

Outside was not like what I just seen. The sky was grey with black clouds. Everything was dry and dead like a wasteland. A white mist traced the ground, whirling around in miniature tornadoes. Everything about this place felt wrong, but nevertheless, I felt compelled to start walking.

I came to a cave and slowly entered, keeping close to the walls. There was an opening lit by blue flames. I peered inside to set my sights on a grotesque creature standing like a guard in front of what looked like a door. The creature had the head of a bull with a huge gold ring through its nose. It had the torso of a very muscular human man, and thick horse legs made of iron. It was wearing a platinum armor breastplate with sleeves around its elbows and shoulders to match, holding a spear in its right hand standing tall. It was massive; I felt a shiver of fear go down my back.

A small hunched creature suddenly walked in. Its skin was covered with fine short hair. It had long, shaggy black hair tumbling down its back and wore a sash around its middle. The troll looked up to the bull-man.

"She will not be pleased once she hears of the escape." Its voice was coarse and cold.

The bull-man glanced down at the troll, huffing out a large breath from its nose. Suddenly, the door behind him began to open and both creatures moved aside to reveal the silhouette of a man standing in the doorway.

I gasped in horror as I sprung up, sitting straight up in my bed. The clock read 9:45pm. Had I really fallen asleep for that long? Covered in sweat and breathing heavily, I laid back on my pillow with relief. It was only a dream. Very rarely did I have such vivid dreams and on top of that, very rarely did my dreams switch from one extreme to the next. One minute I'm in paradise, the next I'm in an underworld.

My stomach grumbled loudly. I could definitely go for those lean and mean steaks now. I got up, took a quick shower to freshen up and made my way downstairs. The family room was empty. I went into the kitchen and found my plate of stir-fried rice with black beans alongside my very juicy steak topped with mushrooms waiting for me on the stove. I put the plate in the microwave and looked outside the patio door. My parents were standing on the porch holding hands, looking up at the sky. I leaned forward to see what they were looking at. The full moon shone brightly, illuminating the sky with its light. I smiled to myself at how cheesy my parents were. It was so typical of them to want to go outside to look at the moon, stars, or even a sunset now and then.

When my food was ready I sat at the table, my stomach growling in anticipation. I quickly devoured my dinner. The patio door was left slightly cracked open, I could hear my parents talking, thinking nothing much of it until I heard Mom raise her voice.

"What do you mean, there's been a breach?"

I looked up in concern. My parents never fought. Dad was still holding Mom's hand as they continued to gaze up at the moon.

"I thought you were the only one with access here, Coral!" Dad's voice was hard and stern.

Coral? What the -? Who are they talking to? From my current position, I couldn't see anyone else in the backyard. I strained to listen to what Coral had to say, but couldn't hear any response.

"What are we supposed to do about this? You know we are useless here." Mom was on the verge of screaming.

After what seemed like a long pause, my parents let go of each other and turned to face one another. Dad put his hands on Mom's shoulders and traced them up to cup her face saying something to her I couldn't make out. Her expression was fearful, although it looked like whatever Dad was saying was beginning to soothe her worry. She closed her eyes nodding her head as he leaned in to kiss her tenderly on the forehead.

They began to walk back to the patio door, freezing instantly when they saw me at the table. I knew then that whatever had taken place between them out there wasn't meant for me to see. Mom marched quickly to the door, sliding it open with force.

"How long have you been here?" Her voice was very stern.

"Relax Mom, I just got here. What's the big deal?" I hoped that my lies would work.

Dad followed closely behind, placing his hand on her shoulder. "Honey, she's trying to have dinner." His voice was soft.

Mom raised her eyebrow, giving me a very curious look.

"What's wrong, Mom? Why are you looking at me like that?"

She finally sighed and sat down at the table next to me. "Nothing, sweetie. I guess I'm just on edge, that's all."

I mimicked her raised eyebrow. "That's not like you?"

"Maybe you should turn in early, honey. How about I go run a nice hot bath for you?" Dad suggested.

Mom smiled back with another sigh. "That would be great, love." She got up and headed upstairs.

"I'm right behind you, honey," Dad called out to her. He turned to me, unease heavy on his face. "Angel, sweetie?"

"Yeah?"

"Have you been noticing anything strange lately?"

"No, why? What's going on?"

He hesitated for a moment, then leaned his elbows on the table and spoke softly. "My father used to always say, 'Listen closely for the night to speak, for you never know when your message will come.' It was his way of saying stay alert." He placed his hand over mine, squeezing it gently. "I need you to keep your eyes open for anything out of the ordinary. Can you do that for me, sweetie?"

His stare was much more serious than his tone, so I nodded my head in reply, feeling confused and anxious.

"Good." He kissed me on the cheek and headed upstairs.

I sat at the table for what felt like forever, trying to wrap my head around what just happened.

Chapter 3: Friend or Foe?

That night I tossed and turned. So many things raced through my mind it was too hard to shut them off. *Who's Coral? What could she have said to upset my parents that much? Is there a kidnapper in the area or something? Why does Dad want me to play investigator?*

Looking up at the ceiling, I finally managed to push those thoughts out of my head, only to allow a whole new wave of thoughts to come in. I hoped that Julie and I could resolve things tomorrow; I know she wasn't one to hold grudges. I brought my arm up to cover my eyes, replaying the scene with Zander in the classroom, groaning at the memory of how terribly awkward I was. Tomorrow had to be a better day. It just had to. After another twenty minutes of rustling, my eyes finally started to get heavy.

* * * * *

Flashes of red and black skies rushed past me. It felt like I was in a time warp catching brief glimpses of things; white lions, an open door with the silhouette of a man, the most horrifying laughter of a woman echoing in the background. It was so sinister I could feel shivers crawling up my skin. Finally the warp ended and I was engulfed in a burst of green lights. I saw my mother reaching for me as if I were a baby in a crib, looking down on me, smiling warmly. My father stood beside her with the same warm expression, his voice a soft echo.

"You're safe now."

I woke up once again gasping, and sat upright in my bed. I looked at the time. It was 6:15am. This was definitely a first, I never woke up before my alarm went off and here I am lying awake in bed with another forty-five minutes to spare. There was no way I was getting back to sleep, so I decided to get ready for the day.

As I walked down the stairs into the kitchen, I vowed to never eat a full meal again before bedtime. I read somewhere once that it's not good to eat big meals close to your bedtime because your body can't digest the food properly and has to fight harder to do so, thus leading to nightmares. I grabbed a bowl and filled it up with Golden Grahams when I heard the sound of footsteps coming from upstairs. Mom came down the stairs in her robe, pausing when she saw me. She rubbed her eyes.

"My eyes must be playing tricks on me! Angel is actually up and dressed before anyone else? Impossible." She smiled playfully, making her way into the kitchen to put on a pot of coffee.

I muffled out a "good morning" through my stuffed mouth. Mom got herself a bowl and came to sit beside me. "So, what's wrong?"

I looked at her cautiously. "Nothing. I couldn't sleep, so I figured I might as well get dressed."

"Hmm." She took in a spoonful of cereal. "What's on your mind?" When I didn't answer she let out a sigh. "Listen, I know I was acting a little off last night, but it's nothing for you to worry about."

Dad came down the stairs, looking at me in disbelief. "You're up? Incredible." They both chuckled to themselves.

Once the humor faded, Mom gave him a concerned look noticing that I wasn't lightening up to their lame joke. Dad sat in front of me at the table with his bowl and poured himself some cereal. He glanced at Mom, then back to me.

"You know you can talk to us, right?"

I looked at them skeptically. I had so many questions, but decided to go with the most basic. "Who's Coral?"

They tensed, looking to each other again. Mom slowly nodded to Dad. He cleared his throat. "Coral is a very good friend from our tribe."

"How much did you hear last night?" Mom's tone wasn't exactly sharp, but wasn't quite relaxed either. She was upset and trying to hide it very poorly.

I didn't respond. They exchanged glances again.

Dad started. "Your mother and I, have some unfinished business we have to deal with."

"What kind of unfinished business?"

"Nothing of concern, sweetie." I could tell he was trying to keep a light smile on his lips.

"You told me that no one except us made it out of our tribe alive. Now all of a sudden you have a good friend? Must be some friend if she was making you both so angry last night." I knew I was overstepping, but they were taking me for a fool. They ask me to talk, then turn around and shut me out. How was that fair?

"Angel, just trust us when we tell you not to worry about it, it's between your mother and I." His tone was soft, but his eyes were cold.

"And obviously Coral." My tone was very cheeky.

Mom glared at me. "This discussion is over. We told you we're handling it, and that is that. I don't want to hear anymore from you." She practically hissed the words out.

I knew that I was fighting a losing battle. Once Mom got all serious, it was game over. She got up and stormed upstairs, Dad following not too long after.

I was furious! I couldn't believe they were acting like kids with their secrets. I didn't say one word to Dad on the way out of the house, nor did I say anything to Mom on the way to school. Once we pulled up she waved at Julie and unlocked the door for me. She was on to my retaliation and decided to play my game. As I got out of the car, Mom kept her gaze straight muttering, "Three thirty, don't be late."

I closed the door and watched as she drove away. Julie slowly made her way over to me and nudged me with her shoulder.

"Hey."

"Hey." I kept staring down the street.

"You and your mom get into a fight or something this morning?"

I turned to face her with a long sigh. "They're keeping something from me and acting all grade one about it." I felt the prickle of tears starting to sting my eyes. Julie put her arm around my shoulder.

"Hey, don't worry about it Angel, I'm sure everything will work out."

I smiled at her, embarrassed. "I'm sorry, I'm just a little fried this morning. I couldn't sleep last night, I kept having these freaky nightmares."

"Eeesh! And we have gym today, so it doesn't look like your nightmare is over yet."

We both laughed. Hearing myself laugh took all my worries away. Julie knew all the tricks to get me to lighten up.

When we got to our lockers, I started to gather up the books I needed for the day, pushing yesterday's books aside. Today was science, gym, geography and math. Julie and I shared all the same classes today except for geography, which was my first class.

"Sorry for having such a big mouth yesterday," Julie said sheepishly, looking at the ground.

"It's OK. I'm sure that's the last thing on my mom's mind right now."

"You didn't get in lots of trouble because of me, did you?"

"Not at all, surprisingly she didn't bring up Zander again."

Julie gasped. "Speaking of, maybe he'll be in more of our classes today?"

I grumbled. "Yeah, maybe. I'm going to start heading over to geo, see you next period."

Once I got to class, Mr. Getty greeted me as he flipped through his textbook. I smiled back and went to sit down, but froze in place when I saw that Zander was in my class. He waved, gesturing for me to sit at the desk beside him. A wave of frigid chills ran through me as I slowly walked over to the empty seat.

"Good morning." His smile was so wide the full power of his beauty hit me like a ton of bricks. I clenched my lips together, forcing myself to smile back before quickly opening my book, bringing it right up to my face to block him from my view. I took in a deep, shuddering breath, realizing that Julie was not in this class, meaning that it was just me, and him. Why did I sit beside him? What was I thinking? With another deep breath, I slowly peered out the side of my book to take a quick peek. He was still staring at me with a subtle grin.

"Everything alright?"

"Mmm hmm," I responded quickly putting the book back up as my shield. *What is wrong with you?* I thought to myself. *If he didn't think you were a freak show yesterday, you're totally making yourself look like a bigger one today!*

Mr. Getty started his lecture on volcanoes and the history behind their formations, giving me the distraction I needed to not focus on how much of a hot mess I was being with this overwhelmingly gorgeous guy next to me.

About halfway through the class, Mr. Getty announced that we will be doing a small project with a partner due two days from now on volcanoes around the world.

"I'll make this easy for everyone. The person to the left of you will be your partner. You have the rest of the class to start discussing the project."

Those words made my heart nearly stop. I slowly peered to my left at Zander.

"Howdy, partner," he smiled.

I gulped hard, once again staring at him like a deer caught in headlights.

"I think we should do the volcano that destroyed the city of Pompeii. It's an epic tragedy," he suggested, getting right down to business.

"Um … yeah, sure," I managed to reply. I had to get a grip, find my voice, and not make myself look like an incompetent fool.

"Excellent." His eyes blazed. "I love that story."

"Why? It's so sad. Everyone was killed."

His eyes lit up with excitement. "That's the beauty of it. They didn't have a chance. It's one of nature's most horrific natural disasters."

"And you consider that beautiful?" It wasn't my intention to undermine his views, but my delivery was definitely less than polite.

"I can see that we're going to get along great," he chuckled.

I felt the heat spread over my cheeks as I smiled bashfully.

"So, any other ideas?" He smiled as he opened his notebook.

As the class went on I began to loosen up, realizing that apart from him being extremely intense and gorgeous, he was actually really cool. We continued planning for the project and decided to meet up at the library tomorrow to do some research. The more we talked, the more comfortable I felt around him, which came as a huge relief.

"Do you have any plans for lunch?" His voice added such depth to the simplest questions.

"Uh, no, Julie and I usually just go to the cafeteria."

"Would it be alright if I joined you?" There was a glimmer in his eyes that made the reddish color really pop.

I reverted back to being a deer in headlights finding it hard to respond.

"Angel?"

"Yeah. Sure." I tried to play off that moment with a coy smile.

"Great." His smile was breathtaking.

I felt my cheeks get hot and began to hastily pack up my books to avoid further embarrassment.

"OK, see you later. Bye!" The words came out faster than an express train, which matched the way I left the classroom. I raised my hand to smack my forehead. I was doing so well and just had to go back to being the freak show again.

When I got to my next class, Julie was already saving me a seat. I slumped down beside her.

"Zander wasn't in my class," she whined.

"Yeah, I know. He was in mine."

Julie's eyes gleamed like two huge marbles. "HE WAS?"

I glanced over at her with a please-don't-start-this-again expression. Instantly she tried to hide her smile and not seem as excited as she clearly was.

"I mean…that's pretty cool. So how was it?"

I didn't want to tell her, but figured she was bound to find out anyways since Zander was joining us at lunchtime.

"If I tell you, you have to promise me you won't make a big deal out of it. OK?"

She sat up straight, raising her right hand as if she were in a courtroom testifying. "I swear!"

"There's this project we have to do and Mr. Getty chose the partners based on the person sitting to your left, so now Zander's my partner and –"

"Wait. You were sitting beside him?" Julie demanded.

I gave her a warning stare. She blushed. "Oops! OK sorry, continue."

I continued my recap of first period, filling her in on all the details she craved. Once she heard that he was having lunch with us, I could see the explosion of excitement bursting inside her.

"Jewls, please don't act all weird at lunch."

"How would I act weird?"

"You'd be so obvious! Giving me looks, nudging me if he said anything that even suggested he liked me. I have a hard enough time trying to talk to him without making myself look stupid, so please just be normal."

"I promise to be on my best behaviour!" Her smile stretched from ear to ear.

I rolled my eyes, smiling back at her.

Throughout the class, I did my best to focus, but my mind was somewhere else. I was not thinking of anything in particular, but found it unusually difficult to follow along with the lecture. I needed to get out of there and take a breather to refocus. I turned to Julie, mouthing to her that I was going to the bathroom.

I made my way out of the classroom and down the empty hallway. I figured that not having a good night's sleep was catching up to me and splashed cold water on my face at the bathroom sink. I gazed at myself in the mirror. I looked pale and drained with dark circles under my eyes.

"Great," I moaned aloud to myself.

A noise came from the stall behind me. I was so sure I was alone when I came in. I continued to look in the mirror, but kept my eyes on the stalls.

There were no visible feet poking out, so I shrugged my shoulders and continued to splash more water on my face.

I glanced up again and froze in horror at the image staring back at me. The pupils in my eyes had shrunken almost completely. My irises were fully dilated and expanded to the point where all the white was practically gone. I gasped in disbelief, watching as fine tanned hairs started to spread across my forehead and under my eyes like a mask. I brought my trembling hands up to touch my face; my fingernails, no longer my own, but sharp black claws. Fear literally paralyzed me. I couldn't even scream. I shut my eyes as tightly as I could.

"It's not real. You're just super tired," I repeated to myself, as I clenched my hands tightly into fists. My heart thrashed painfully in my chest.

Slowly, I opened my eyes again, exhaling gratefully at the discovery of just plain old me staring back. I immediately brought my hands up. They too had gone back to normal. I let out another huge breath, bringing my now shaky hands to cup my forehead.

"I *must* have caught something."

Another rustling came from the stall again and this time I turned to face the disturbance. A faint animalistic growl sounded from behind the closed door in front of me. My mouth went dry as I continued to stare at the stall door, telling myself over and over that I was imagining things again. The only way to prove this to myself was to investigate. Slowly and shakily, I forced myself to walk towards the stall. I took in a deep breath and lightly pushed the door open. Nothing. I stood transfixed in front of the empty stall for what felt like an eternity.

The bathroom door swung open and Julie came walking in.

"You've been in here forever! What are you doing? There's a ton of notes that you have to copy from me now!"

Julie noticed my startled appearance and paused. "You OK?"

I continued to stand in front of the empty stall with my head turned to her. So many emotions were going through me. Relief. Fear. Shock. What could

I say to her? That I was seeing things? Hearing things? I managed to choke out, "I'm not feeling well."

"Yeah, I can tell. You look like crap." She gave me a concerned smile and put her arm around my shoulders. "Do you want me to come with you to the office and call your mom?"

That was another thing I did not want to deal with. As much as I thought I was losing my mind, there's no way I was going to get interrogated from my suddenly secretive parents.

"No, I think I just need some rest and maybe some lunch."

I then remembered that Zander was having lunch with us, bringing on another wave of stress.

"Well, we only have fifteen minutes left of class, so we should head back. Ms. Joanings sent me to look for you. But before we go, we need to do something with your face. You seriously do look like crap, babe."

Julie put her little purse on the sink and took out a mini spray bottle, some blush and some lipgloss. "Here, spray this on your face. It's a revitalizer, it'll give you a cute glow." With a few sprays, a little dab of blush and lip-gloss, Julie's makeover was complete and I was back to looking like a member of the living again." Perfecto! Now let's go." She grabbed my arm, smiling in satisfaction at her successful makeover.

As we walked back to class, I tried my hardest to forget what had just happened, but I found myself on guard, glancing around nervously in anticipation for something else to happen. When we got back to class, Ms. Joanings called me over to her desk to ask if everything was alright. I quickly made up a story that I wasn't feeling well and had to wander the halls to see if anyone had any Aspirin, resulting in me going to the office to get some from the nurse. Although, after that whole scene in the bathroom I was thinking I might actually need that Aspirin sooner than later if this day continued on this way.

Ms. Joanings gave me a nod of understanding and I made my way back to my desk, which was full of notes. Julie wasn't kidding! These notes were enough for an entire week, much less one period, so for the remainder of the period I sat copying as much as I could, but knew I would have to take it home.

"Angel, c'mon! We have to get to the cafeteria, we don't want to keep him waiting!" Jewls hurried me impatiently.

"Jewls, the bell hasn't even gone yet. Relax!"

She stood up, looking at me like I was a dunce. "The bell rang like five minutes ago. You were too caught up in the glamor of note taking to notice, I guess."

I gazed around the empty classroom, turned back to Julie to give her a shamefaced smile, got up, packed my stuff and headed back to our lockers.

As I hung up my backpack, a stinging chill swept over me. The feeling was so sharp I yelped as my body stiffened, shocking me with its needle-like sensations.

Julie quickly slammed her locker to look at me. "What happened?"

I barely registered that she was speaking; the chill was still running through me. My ears started ringing when I realized in horror that I had no control over my body. Something was taking over my senses, steering me around to face the hallway. I bumped into Zander so hard, the impact made me fall back. He managed to catch me with both hands gripping my shoulders firmly.

"Whoa, careful," he grinned, his eyes concerned.

"What the hell was that?" Julie's mouth was wide open in disbelief. "You practically ran him over!"

Finally, the ringing in my ears stopped. I looked to Julie with wide eyes, then to Zander feeling mortified. What was *wrong* with me!

"I'm so sorry, I don't know what just happened."

He slowly released me. "It's OK. It's my fault, really, I should have said something."

"Don't mind Angel, she's not feeling very well today." Jewls began leading Zander down the hallway, looking back at me mouthing GET IT TOGETHER before turning back to him. "How about we get some grub in her before she tackles some other poor soul?"

They chuckled at my expense and I gave them an awkward smile before swiftly turning back to grab my wallet from the locker.

"Oh my god! Could this day get any worse?" I whispered to myself. I wanted to cry, I was beyond embarrassed, but there was no time for a pity party. The faster I got today over with, the better.

The cafeteria was usually packed, but today it seemed as if everyone wanted to be outside; the weather was perfect. The field was filled with students sitting on benches or on the lawn chatting away. Zander and Julie suggested that we too should enjoy the outdoors, so we found a spot under a couple of trees near the track that we settled under. The breeze was warm and refreshing. I glanced over at Julie who could not stop smiling, thrilled that Zander actually wanted to hang out with us. He was leaning up against the tree with his arms crossed. If ever someone could be described as perfect, it would be him. As the sun broke through the clouds, lighting up his face, the reddish color in his eyes became more enhanced, making them appear almost ruby-like. He grabbed a pair of dark aviator shades out of his pocket and put them on.

"So, what do you guys like to do for fun?" He looked over at Julie, then tilted his head toward me.

"Well, Angel and I usually hit up the movies or the mall. The closest and only one worth going to is the Eaton Centre, it's huge. Unless you prefer vintage or independent shops, then Kensington Market is pretty sweet. A drive-in theatre actually opened up three weeks ago, they've got mini golf, roller skating and a cute little restaurant, so that has kind of been a hot spot." Julie was beaming, loving every second of filling him in on all the hot spots, latest gossip, and good restaurants. She was the ultimate guide to all things Toronto.

I sat back listening to her ramble on and was intrigued to see how fascinated Zander was with all of it. He was genuinely interested. He wanted to know everything, like a sponge just soaking up as much information as he could.

"So tell me, Angel, what is your background?" Zander asked, interrupting my daydreams.

"African."

He leaned forward, intrigued. "African, huh?"

"What, you don't believe me?"

"No, it's not that, I just never would have guessed. So, are you and your family close?"

"Yeah, very close! All my life it's just been the three of us. We have no other family here."

"No?"

"Yeah, there were riots in the village where my parents lived, so they had to leave."

His eyebrows rose in astonishment. "Wow. I guess there's no going back?"

"I doubt it. Although recently they seem to have gotten back in touch with this woman who's apparently from their tribe. Someone named Coral."

Zander tensed, clenching his lips together in a tight line.

"Something wrong?" I asked.

His face instantly reverted back to being calm and intrigued.

"Nah, I just had a cramp in my back is all. So, that's great then that they've reconnected with a friend."

I involuntarily rolled my eyes. "I guess."

"You don't seem very thrilled about it."

"Angel's just pissed because her parents are keeping some secret from her," Julie blurted out, taking a huge chomp out of her sandwich.

My eyes bugged in shock as I glared at Julie.

Zander caught every moment of it. He placed his hand over his chest. "I'm sorry, it's none of my business."

"No, it's fine, I guess I just didn't expect Jewls to say that."

She looked at me, realizing her big mouth just got her in trouble again. "Oops."

"So what gives you the impression you're being kept in the dark?

"Well, they're usually very open about everything, but last night when I overheard them talking with Coral, they got pretty upset with her. I asked them about it this morning, but they got all defensive and shut me out."

Zander sat very still, his jaw clenched. "Do you have any idea what they were talking about?"

"No."

He stared back at me in such a strange way. It almost felt as if he was trying to determine if I was telling the truth or not.

"What about you, Zander, where is your family from?" Julie asked in her bubbly tone.

"Well, my father was born and raised in Rome, and my mother in Greece. That's where they met, actually."

"Aww, nice. Is that where you were raised?"

He turned and smiled at Julie, almost putting her in a daze. "Um, I think so."

"You think so?" I asked, puzzled.

Zander chuckled. "Sounds weird, huh? But to be honest, I don't really remember much of my childhood. My parents said I was very ill when I was a kid, near death actually."

"Oh no!" Julie gasped dramatically.

He flashed her a wide smile. "As you can see, I did recover. My parents brought me to a hospital in Seattle where we lived for quite some time. I don't remember living in Greece at all."

"Thank God you went to that hospital." Julie's enthusiasm was starting to nauseate me.

"You're not hungry?" I asked Zander once I noticed he hadn't eaten anything.

"No, I ate earlier, I had a spare after first period so I'm on a double lunch."

I continued to scarf down my fries, listening as Julie continued to monopolize the conversation, going into detail about our school and the teachers. I decided to lie down and soak up the sun while they chatted away.

Lunch passed by very quickly. With the weather being so amazing, it seemed like no time would be enough to spend outside. On the way back to our lockers, Zander walked beside me, brushing my shoulder with his.

"You've been very quiet. Still not feeling well?" He took off his glasses, putting them back in his pocket. His eyes expressed genuine concern.

"Yeah. Sorry. I think I'm coming down with something."

"Did you still want to meet up tomorrow? I could come over after school?" He smiled warmly.

He must have lost his mind to think that would even be an option. Mom would kill me if I had a boy in the house, especially the boy she knows is into me, thanks to Julie's big mouth.

"Um, I don't think that would be a good idea. My parents are very protective, especially when it comes to guys."

"Oh." He seemed surprised.

"But I could ask my mom to drop me off at school early tomorrow so that we can get some research in first thing, and then maybe again at lunch?"

"That would be perfect."

"Great." Realizing I was giving him a very googly-eyed stare, I cleared my throat. "Well, see you tomorrow then."

The rest of the day I had to deal with Julie's constant admiration of how amazing Zander is and how she's so happy we got to hang out with him. I felt like rolling my eyes at her, but resisted against it, deciding to focus my energy on the fact that I felt a lot better than I did this morning. I tried to make sense of the scene in the bathroom, but I couldn't. Was I really that sleep-deprived that I would imagine something that crazy? What other explanation could there be? I settled on my lack of sleep being the reason and decided that I would have to catch up tonight for sure.

After school, Julie and I rushed back to the parking lot to make sure that my mom would not be in a worse mood than she was this morning. Surprisingly, once we got in the car, her mood was extra cheerful.

"Good afternoon ladies!" Julie and I glanced cautiously at each other. "Isn't this weather absolutely amazing?"

"Geez, Mrs. Seriki, you're awfully happy."

"Of course I am; why wouldn't I be? I get to pick up my two favorite girls. I was thinking we could go out to the boardwalk and grab something to eat by the lake, just us girls."

"What about, Dad?"

"He's working overtime on his new painting, he won't be back from the gallery for a couple of hours." She was practically giggling. "Oh, and how could I forget, my sweetheart is turning seventeen in less than two weeks! We have a party to plan."

"Yes!" Julie wailed in excitement. "See, Angel, I told you it's a big deal!"

My mouth hung open in shock. Who was this woman and what has she done with my mother? Obviously Julie couldn't tell how incredibly wrong this was. She took the bait! All Mom had to do was say party and Julie was officially in Wonderland. I, on the other hand, knew better. Mom was not one for parties or the planning for that matter, and since when were we referred to as her favorite girls? She was up to something and I knew it.

"OK, whoa, slow down! Mom, you never mentioned anything to me before about wanting to throw me a party and as I said before, I don't want one."

"Don't listen to her Mrs. Seriki."

Mom turned to wink at Julie, then turned back to me. "Angel, honey, I know I'm not the biggest fan of the whole party scene, but seventeen is a milestone for us."

"Yeah, I know, I just don't want to make a big deal out of it."

"How about we all grab something to eat? I have a blanket in the back, we can have a little picnic and talk more about it?" She caressed the side of my cheek and softly grabbed my chin, "C'mon, Angel-baby, lighten up."

"Yeah! Lighten up!" Julie teased.

I slumped in my seat, crossing my arms. "Fine."

Mom began to pull away when she suddenly slammed on the brakes. Julie and I lurched forward. Thank God we had on our seatbelts or we would have been bugs on the windshield. I turned bewildered to look at Mom. She was gripping the steering wheel so hard her knuckles were losing all color. She quickly started scanning the parking lot, then turned to look out the passenger window.

"Mom, what is it?" Concern was thick in my voice.

She ignored me and continued to scan frantically until her eyes locked in place and narrowed. I followed her gaze to see what she was looking at. The front of the school was crowded with kids. A tingling cold breeze brushed past me as I spotted Zander, walking with his back to us heading back inside the school.

Chapter 4: Unknown Territory

I watched Mom warily until she put the car back into drive and pulled away from the school. She didn't say a single word, the atmosphere instantly changing from vibrant and happy to tense.

"Mrs. Seriki, is everything alright?"

"Fine." Mom responded back to Julie through clenched teeth. She was still gripping the wheel just as tightly.

Julie shot me a puzzled look and threw up her shoulders. I couldn't believe that Mom was just going to act as if she didn't just have a spaz attack. Was she looking at Zander? Did he see her glaring at him? Was that why he was walking away? I would be scared to death too if I got that look from my mother. Could she know that, that *was the* Zander? I knew she was protective, but could she be trying to scare him off? Great! All I need is to be single forever thanks to my darling mother who likes to act like she's in the secret service, specializing in assassination!

"Mom, what gives? You could've given us a warning or something!"

She glanced at me from the corner of her eye and slowly started to loosen her grip on the wheel. "Sorry, girls, I just thought I recognized someone."

"Well, that's quite the look to give them if you did!" Julie laughed.

Mom smiled slightly. "Well, it wasn't necessarily someone I was especially pleased to see." She took in a deep breath and put back on her bubbly façade.

If there was ever a time to be confused, it was now. I didn't know exactly who she was staring at, but I had a sneaking suspicion that it was Zander.

Once we got to the boardwalk, Julie and I found a spot on the sand to lay out the blanket while Mom went to order burgers and fries. She brought back a whole bag full of goodies: double chocolate macadamia nut cookies, caramel popcorn, and sour gummies along with huge burgers, fries and shakes. My mom wasn't necessarily a health freak, but she did prefer to eat more natural and organic foods, so this was a real treat. Since she was back in her cheery mood, Julie was all over her about the party planning.

"I was telling Angel before that this birthday party should be huge! Maybe like a backyard luau with a bonfire!"

"Oooohh! That sounds like so much fun!" Mom gushed. "But if we are going to have a bonfire, why not show our heritage? Angel has always loved the paintings of the fire rituals back in our village that her father made. The costumes are so cute, you two would look so good in them! We could have drummers come in and put on a little show. What do you say, sweetie?"

I admit I was beginning to be swayed. The thought of a tribal-themed party was interesting, but I wasn't sold on huge. "It sounds like fun, I just don't want a lot of people there. It's my birthday and I should have a say, no?"

"Absolutely." Mom winked at Julie.

"Then I'll agree to this party if you guys agree to my conditions."

"Conditions?" Julie raised her eyebrows.

"Yes, conditions. I only want close friends and family, which is pretty much four people, maybe a few more, but that's it! I don't want more than ten people! If turning seventeen is all that special, why should I have a bunch of people around me that I barely talk to?"

Mom, who'd been sucking on a sour gummy, looked to Julie for approval. Julie nodded. "It's settled, then," Mom said. "We're having a party, and you two can decide who to invite to our VIP event."

Julie shrieked in excitement, clapping her hands together. "Wait." She paused, looking cautiously at my mom. "Are boys allowed?"

Mom pursed her lips and raised her eyebrows. We always called it her "diva look". "Boys, huh? I guess that would be OK."

Julie's shriek went up another two octaves in excitement. Mom laughed and rolled her eyes as I sat in astonishment. This was a moment in history.

We sat there soaking up as much sun as we could, eating and planning out the details of the décor. We would have Tiki torches lit throughout the backyard, and focus on green, red, orange and white as the colour scheme. Our outfits would consist of brown suede skirts and black halter-tops. There would be seashells everywhere and Mom would bring out her huge drum set she had gotten at an antique store. By the time the sun was setting, I had fully caught on to the excitement and giddiness that Julie and Mom were radiating. Despite the run-in that my Mom and I had this morning, I was really enjoying our girl's night out. It was very relaxing to be laid out on a blanket facing the water, listening to the sounds of the waves hitting the shore and feeling the warm breeze tickle my cheeks.

But as much as I wanted to forget everything that has been happening, I had to find out what my parents were hiding, and why Mom was trying so hard to put on this show like everything was fine. I stared at her as she laughed, playing rock paper scissors with Julie over the last sour gummy. I loved seeing her so happy and realized at that moment how terrified I actually was at the thought of anything bad happening to her or Dad. She was a very strong woman, I knew she could handle just about anything, but it was evident how upset she was last night about whatever secret they were hiding. I had to find out, it was more than curiosity - it was a need. I needed to know that my parents would be ok.

The sun had nearly disappeared below the distant horizon, so we started packing up. Mom dropped off Julie and we sat in silence the rest of the way home, enjoying each other's company, listening to the radio.

As we pulled into the driveway, Mom seemed to be in a rush to get inside. Dad was sitting in the kitchen still wearing his work apron with an unsettled look on his face. He always had this grace about him; his features were very defined with his squared jawline, broad forehead and pointed nose in contrast to his smooth chocolate brown hair. He wasn't very muscular, but he had a decent build. People always said he should be an actor because he carries himself with such poise and style. I personally thought he looked like John Stamos with the exception of his eyes. He seemed startled as I closed the door behind us, as if he'd just lost a very serious train of thought. He rose from his seat, flashing us a wide smile that didn't quite touch his eyes.

"Hey, guys! How was girls night?" He sounded just as chipper as Mom had earlier.

Mom walked ahead of me to greet Dad and I noticed their eye contact as a signal. Mom stretched and yawned, claiming that she was pooped after such a fun-filled evening and that she was going to start getting ready for bed. Dad then conveniently glanced at the time and said that he too should get cleaned up since he was covered in paint. He turned to kiss me on the forehead.

"Goodnight honey. We'll have to catch up in the morning."

I knew there was no hope in getting any information from Mom, but I had some faith that I could get Dad to talk. I waited until Mom was upstairs to confront Dad and catch him before he was at the foot of the stairs.

"Hey, Dad?"

"Yes, sweetie?"

"Can I talk to you for a minute? It's kind of important."

He glanced up the stairs with a look of indecision, then back to me. "Is everything alright?"

I motioned for him to come and sit by patting the bar stool beside mine. He glanced one more time up the stairs, exhaled, then walked over with a concerned look on his face. "What's up?"

I took in a deep breath. This was not going to be easy. I was no good at confrontations. I always got so emotional. I spoke very low so that Mom wouldn't overhear.

"You asked me last night if I'd noticed anything strange going on, and I have."

He leaned forward, stiff with anticipation. "What kind of things?"

"I know Dad. I know you and Mom are keeping something very important from me. I can see through your charade and silent signals to each other. Now tell me what's going on. Are you guys in trouble?"

Dad clenched his jaw. "Angel, sweetie, we told you –"

"I know what you told me!" I tried to lower my voice again while giving him a cold stare. "I'm not a kid anymore, Dad, I know when I'm being lied to."

He stared back at me with an agonized expression before he smiled warmly. Lighting up his entire face, his eyes were practically gleaming.

"Angel, sweetie, why are you getting so worked up? We're not in trouble. You don't have to worry."

I continued to stare blankly. "Really? If there's nothing to worry about, why can't you tell me what the issue is?"

Dad chuckled. "You know how your mother gets, she's a firecracker. We were caught a little off guard with some unexpected news, but everything is fine, I promise."

"It doesn't *look* like it's fine. I saw your face when I came in here; you're upset about something, even though you're doing a pretty good job at hiding it right now. Something is wrong."

His eyes were soft. "Angel, nothing is wrong, OK?"

I stared at him, trying to determine whether he was genuine or not, but couldn't. His eyes were honest. I plopped my head onto my folded arms on the table with a loud sigh.

"Sweetie, you look exhausted. Stop worrying and try to get a good night's sleep, will you?"

"Ugh. You're impossible."

He kissed my forehead and headed upstairs with another, "Don't worry, everything's fine."

I sat perplexed, feeling a lump in my throat that I couldn't swallow. I wanted to believe him, but everything inside me was screaming that it was all a front. But why would he lie to me? It didn't make sense.

I forced myself to move and make my way to my room. I had to relax, my heart was racing and my stomach was twisting. I tried to be really quiet as I got to the top of the stairs, waiting to see if I could listen in on their conversation. I knew they were talking, but the bathtub faucet was running water so it was hard to hear anything. I needed to get closer. I took another step forward, leaning against the wall by their door. I couldn't make out anything Mom was saying, it was all muffled. Dad responded with something else that I couldn't make out. It was useless. My stomach continued to twist in knots at the thought of being lied to by my own parents, the two people who should never lie to me. I took in a deep breath, telling myself to drop it and made my way back to my room.

I threw myself onto my bed in frustration. I had to get some sleep tonight, today had been way too crazy and I wasn't looking for this to be repeated tomorrow. My thoughts started to wander as I lay looking up at the ceiling, taking me back to last night when I heard the distress in Mom's voice. I forced myself to think of something else as I felt the lump clench in my throat. Happy thoughts, like my party. I was thrilled that Mom was on board, even though it wasn't going to be big. I had a secret love for themed parties and this one gave me butterflies in a good way.

I wished that things were different for my family; that we could actually go back and visit the place my parents grew up in and loved so much. I wished I could have gotten to experience all the heritage, and the stories that came along with the village. This party would be the closest thing to celebrating my heritage that I could get. Julie would be all over me tomorrow about our VIP list of boys (*I still can't believe it!*) and others that were considered good friends.

Maybe Tamara from my English class and June from history, they were pretty cool and occasionally joined Julie and I for lunch. I would definitely have to invite Joss: Julie's first-grade crush for her flirting benefits, and Hector, my wonderful brother from another mother. I've known Hector as long as Julie, we were very close. He moved to British Columbia three years ago. We've always kept in touch. In fact, I was positive that he would be thrilled to hear about my new "friend". Although he hasn't officially come out to the rest of the world yet, Hector confided in me last year that he thinks he might be gay, which totally fit. I remember when we were kids he would always come up to Julie and I during recess and ask if we were going to play Barbies after school, calling dibs on Ariel.

The memory brought a smile to my face, which was short-lived as the lump in my throat began clenching again. I knew Julie would demand that Zander be on the list, but as much as I would love for him to come to my party, it terrified me for two reasons. One: Mom. She would serve his head on a platter if she saw for herself the way he looks at me. The more I thought about what happened in the car after school today, the more I realized that it didn't make sense for it to have been Zander that she was glaring at. She said that she thought she'd recognized someone and Zander was new to the school, so it had to have been someone else. And two: I was still not a hundred percent comfortable around him. I hoped that that would change with us working on this project together. It actually surprises me that I haven't scared him off yet with me acting like such a dork around him. It began to make me wonder. Could I actually have a chance with him?

Chapter 5: True or False

I woke up in a cold sweat, breathing heavily. Another nightmare. This one wasn't as vivid as the others, but far more jumbled. There were figures that seemed to merge together with congested sounds, as if too many people were trying to talk at once. Once the haze stopped, I found myself alone in a room with the same silhouette of a man from my previous dreams.

I looked over at the clock: 3:30am. I headed downstairs for some water. As I was pouring myself a glass, a thick white fog began to form around me. I froze in place, my heart pounding so hard it made my eardrums hurt. I wanted to move, to run, but I couldn't. I was stuck, locked in place by this unknown force that continued to circle me. A faint whisper caressed my ear.

"She's coming for you."

Horrified and trembling uncontrollably, I forced myself to speak through chattering teeth. "W-Wh-Who are you?"

"She's close," the voice hissed, and then faster than it had appeared, the fog dissipated into nothing.

I let out a gush of air, unable to hold back tears from streaming down my face. I brought my hands up to my chest, trying to calm myself down by taking in long, deep breaths. There was no excuse I could think of this time. This was *real*. Something was happening to me. Something supernatural. I composed myself enough to turn around with the intention of running to my parents' room, but there stood the same dark figure at the other end of the kitchen, watching me. I screamed and everything went dark.

I awoke in my bed and jolted upright in a cold sweat. Shaking violently, I touched my bed, my pillows, my face and looked at the clock which read 3:30am. Had I dreamed it all? Watching myself wake up from a dream within a dream? It felt too real. The others had been vivid, yes, but *this*? This time was real. Wasn't it?

I wanted to cry, but couldn't. What was happening to me? I had cleared my head enough before I went to sleep and I ate hours before. This wasn't stress, right? I didn't know what to tell myself, or what to believe anymore. If my mind was playing tricks on me, this was a heavy-duty upgrade from tricks to hallucinations. I ran my fingers through my damp hair and started to pray.

"Dear God, help me. There's a darkness lingering around me. Show me what to do." I opened my eyes and froze at the memory of the words my father spoke to me last night and spoke them aloud to myself. "The night. It's *speaking*."

Everything clicked. This whole time I was convinced that Dad was keeping secrets when he was really trying to show me, or guide me to the truth. He told me about his father's saying: "When the night speaks I must listen." Well it spoke all right! Someone was coming for me, a woman. But who? Coral? What does she want from me? I wanted more than anything to burst into my parents' room and tell Dad what the night had revealed to me, but I couldn't. This wasn't about my parents. It was about me. I had to deal with this somehow, figure it out. My parents had been through enough; I would never be able to live with myself knowing that they were facing danger because of me. Because I was too much of a coward to face whatever this was myself. I reached over to my end table, grabbed my diary out of the drawer and began jotting down the facts that I knew.

1. Nightmares – signs or signals?
2. Cold sensations – warning?

But if number two was indeed a warning … I always had the chills whenever Zander was around. Could that mean that he's dangerous? At this point, anything was a potential threat.

3. Zander – friend or foe?
4. The dark figure – what does it mean?
5. Coral – how can I get to her before she gets to me?

Dad had said the other night that she was a friend from their tribe. So if this was true, I had nothing to worry about. But if it was false … well, I guess I'd find out soon enough. I remembered that it was a full moon, which usually lasts for three nights. Maybe that was her signal to my parents to come out and she would be there. The idea made sense. For as far back as I could remember, my parents always went out on the back porch during a full moon to look at the stars. Or so they said. Maybe this whole time they were talking to Coral?

I got up out of bed, walked over to my window, and pulled back the drapes. The moon shone bright as ever in the sky. Indecision plagued me. Should I do this? Can I do this? I picked up whatever clothes were on the floor by my closet, threw them on and headed downstairs out the back door.

The air was warm, but cool enough to make me fold my arms across my chest for warmth. I looked up at the sky. It was another clear night. The sky was a vast ocean of stars with a bright pearl-shaped full moon. It was beautiful.

Well, I thought. *Here goes nothing.* I tried to make myself sound stern so that if I were to get an answer back, she wouldn't detect any fear in my voice.

"Coral?" I spoke to the night sky. "Coral, are you there?"

I waited. Nothing.

"Listen, if you're there, I need answers! I need to know what's happening! Show me a sign!"

Silence.

Ugh! I raged. *This was useless! No, ludicrous is more the word I'm looking for. What the hell am I doing outside in the middle of the night, talking to who? Coral, my imaginary friend! Why would I even believe that she'd be here? This is so stupid!* I turned on my heels in frustration and there Dad stood, leaning up against the doorframe.

"Dad!" I gasped. "Wh-What are you doing up?"

I tried to decipher if the expression on his face was anger, suspicion or sadness. He continued to gaze at me, speaking softly with a cold undertone. "I should be asking *you* that. What exactly are you doing out here, Angel?"

"I – I was just –"

"Just talking to yourself?" He narrowed his eyes at me. He knew what I was doing.

I swallowed hard. "I was trying to listen, Dad."

"Listen to what?"

I exhaled loudly. "To the night speaking."

We both stood staring at each other, saying absolutely nothing. He pinched the bridge of his nose and blew out an exasperated breath. "Come here."

I walked towards him and he pulled me into an embrace, holding me tightly. Again I wanted to cry, but couldn't. He kissed the top of my head,

"Let's keep this between us, OK, sweetie?"

I squeezed him tighter. "OK, Dad."

He broke the embrace to cup my face in his hands, his eyes distressed. "What did the night say to you?"

I tried to mask my dumbfounded expression. I wasn't crazy after all. This is what he wanted me to do. I wanted to tell him about the threat from my dream, but decided to keep that to myself. It wasn't technically lying if I only answered the question based on my attempt to talk to Coral, and not my earlier encounter. "Nothing."

His eyes searched mine for truth. He seemed to accept my answer. "Come on, let's get inside huh? Tomorrow's still a school day and at this rate, it may be difficult to get you up." He gave me a weary smile.

I returned his smile half-heartedly and followed him back inside.

* * * * *

Mom dropped me off in front of the school as usual, but Dad's predictions were right. I was late. Class started a half hour ago and Mom was not impressed with my unwillingness to get out of bed. If only she knew that I got about three hours of sleep, if that. My eyes burned and every limb in my body felt like it weighed a hundred pounds. I peeled myself out of the front seat and attempted to speed walk to my locker.

The hallways were empty and filled only with the sounds of my dragging feet. I yawned loudly while twiddling my lock when I was hit with a chill that made my hairs tingle all over my body. This time it only took about two seconds for the initial shock to wear off. I knew who it was.

"You know, you really shouldn't sneak up on people like that, Zander." I mumbled in a monotone without turning to face him.

I continued to gather my books together when I realized he hadn't responded. I turned around slowly. Zander stood on the other side of the hallway, leaning against the lockers with his hands in his dark denim jean pockets, giving me a sly grin. A lock of hair hung over his face, coming to rest by his auburn eyes, which seemed to glow a brownish red against his burnt orange V-neck sweater. He was by far the most gorgeous guy I'd ever seen. Instantly I felt a rush of adrenaline and caught my second wind. My heart started to race and I tried my best to play it cool.

"No hello?" I chuckled nervously.

He continued to stare at me with that sly grin and took his hands out of his pockets to cross them against his chest. "How did you know it was me?"

I felt the blood rush to my cheeks. "Uh, lucky guess."

"Very lucky." His eyes burned into mine. "You know, it's very damaging to one's ego when they've been stood up."

"Stood up? Who stood you –"

Oh crap. I completely forgot about my rendez-vous that we'd arranged for this morning to work on our project. I slapped my palm against my forehead. "Oh my gosh, I am so sorry! I totally forgot all about it! I didn't get a lot of sleep last night, so I'm a little brain-dead today."

He slowly leaned forward, started walking over and stopped about a foot in front of me, tilting his head to one side. "What kept you up?"

His cologne had a deep vanilla and wood mix. It smelled incredible, and he was close. *Too* close. I took a couple steps back to give myself a comfortable distance from him, but he followed, closing the gap until I was against my locker with him still being a foot away. I couldn't find words in that moment; I was completely hypnotized by his eyes. It was as if there was an electric charge surging through me as I took in his gorgeous features: the way his hair rested beside his eyes, his full lips, the faint dimples that formed when he smiled.

"Earth to Angel," he grinned as he leaned one hand against the lockers beside my head.

"I'm sorry, what did you say?"

FOCUS, ANGEL! FOCUS! I berated myself.

His full smile literally made my knees wobble. "You must be really tired, huh?"

"Yeah, I … I'm sorry. I guess I must still be waking up."

"We'll just have to make up for this morning after school. If you're not doing anything that is."

"Sure, yeah, I'll just tell Julie I won't be going home with her today and let my mom know I'll be late." *Julie is going to freak when she hears this one,* I thought.

"Perfect." His eyes searched mine. "So, we still on for lunch?"

"Mmm hmmm."

He finally leaned back, creating more distance between us. "Great. See you then." He began to walk down the hallway, turning back to me just before he turned the corner. "Oh, Angel?"

"Yeah?"

"You should hurry, class is done in twenty minutes." He chuckled and kept walking.

I let out a long breath. That was *intense*! I debated whether or not to tell Julie. I was on such a high that her giddy and outrageous over-excitement wouldn't bother me this time. I let out a little squeal, biting down on my lip to contain my smile, closed my locker and headed to class.

Ms. Foster was not impressed with my tardiness. Class was pretty much over, and everyone had been taking notes for the last ten minutes. Thankfully, Julie already had notes prepared for me.

"Ho-ly! Late much?" Julie leaned over from her desk. "What gives?"

"I overslept. Like, a *lot*."

"You do look like you just rolled out of bed," Julie chuckled.

I made a face at her. "Gee, thanks."

She leaned in even closer, making sure only I could hear her. "Did you have another nightmare?"

I nodded.

"Geez, Angel, that's every night now. Was it the same one?"

"No, this one was even worse. I saw myself waking up after a nightmare, getting something to drink and the silhouette of a man was *in the kitchen* with me! Then I woke up." I watched as concern set Julie's face into a frown. "And that's not even the worst of it. In the dream, something spoke to me, telling me someone was coming for me and that she was close."

Her eyes bulged. "She? A woman? Angel, this is getting bad. I'm worried about you."

"Jewls, I'm way too tired to talk about this anymore, it just makes my head hurt." I let out a breath, and tried to lighten the mood, giving her a devious smile. "You are going to legit *die* when I tell you about my encounter with Zander this morning!"

Instantly, her eyes lit up and she rubbed her hands together. "Tell me! Tell me! Tell me!"

I gave her the entire play-by-play leaving no rock unturned and for a second I thought she stopped breathing. Her mouth hung open. I had rendered her speechless.

The bell rang for next period.

"O-M-G!" she squealed. "So you mean to tell me that after *all* that up-close-and-personal stuff, you're just going to *casually* go spend lunch together and then an hour after school with him as if *nothing happened*? You guys are *totally* gonna kiss! Wait, no. Not with the way you explained this energy between you two. You're gonna make out!" She started bouncing in her giddy strides as we walked back to our lockers.

"Are you nuts? That is NOT happening! I barely know the guy."

"Well, it sure does look like you're in for a whole lot of quality time. Quick, come with me!"

Julie dragged me into the bathroom and gave me another one of her quick makeovers, along with a pep talk on kissing. As much as I tried to cut her off, she just kept talking over me and driving her points home. Julie was more experienced than I was as she had already kissed two guys. Her first kiss was with her first boyfriend, Frankie, back in grade eight at our grad dance. After only two months she swore he was the guy she was destined to marry until she found him locking lips with another girl that summer.

Then there was Armando, an exchange student from Panama last year who she was dared to kiss at a party, and ended up making out with for the rest of the night. She claimed it "just happened". They ended up becoming really good friends until he had to go back to Panama after two months. I had to listen to her go on and on and *on* about him every day for the rest of the year. She was convinced that she was cursed with only two months of happiness when it came to anyone she liked.

I on the other hand, had not officially had my first kiss yet. Last year at that same party where Julie met Armando, this guy who was *not* at all my type was dared to kiss *me*. I told him that my mother would hunt him down and kill him, so he settled for giving me a sloppy wet kiss on the cheek instead. Ugh, the memory alone sent chills up my spine. He was so gross! But, the thought of *Zander* kissing me... now that was a whole different story! How would I know what the hell to do? Julie says that I'll just know and it will happen naturally, but knowing my luck, I'd do or say something stupid to ruin the moment. Our encounters were weird enough on their own with the chills he gave me. I still had to dig deeper into that and figure out if he's Mr. Right or Mr. Wrong.

* * * * *

After history, I waited for Zander just outside of the cafeteria. It was getting harder to keep my eyes open, my eyelids were so heavy. If I was going to get through the rest of the day I needed a serious hit of caffeine, so I settled on a Cola from the pop machine. As I was grabbing the change out of my wallet, a chill hit me. I smiled to myself, realizing that instead of thinking this 'thing' I kept feeling deemed me a freak of nature, I could use it to my advantage.

"Hey, did you want one too?" I asked my new visitor, still facing the pop machine. "Zander?"

"How do you keep doing that?" Zander asked with that low raspy voice.

I cracked open my pop, taking a big gulp as I turned to face him with a smug smile. "Magic."

"So I guess it wasn't just a lucky guess after all. Careful, I just may have a few tricks of my own." The corner of his lips lifted in a slight smile. "So, should we head over to the library?"

"Uh, yeah. Shouldn't we get a quick bite first?" My stomach had been growling all morning.

"I had a big breakfast, I'm not hungry."

"Oh, ok. I'll just get something fast then from the caf because trust me without it, already being tired, I could become very dangerous." I chuckled.

He smirked. "Believe me, I know the feeling."

I quickly got a bagel with cream cheese and we headed over to the library. There was a spot by the windows in the far back corner that we decided to settle into. My nerves started to kick in once I realized that we were alone. Surprisingly, Zander was all business. We got most of our project on Pompeii finished just as the bell rang. I was actually quite relieved at how well we worked together. I thought he would've been bossy or even a bit of a snob since he went to Eastern Mills. His knowledge on the entire subject was remarkable. I had to give him credit.

He walked me back to my locker, discussing the final pieces we should look for after school in the library. I caught Julie's wide smile as we turned the corner.

"Hey guys! How was lunch?" Julie casually nudged me with her elbow.

Zander smiled back politely to Julie. "Very productive."

He casually placed his hand on the small of my back. A burst of what felt like electricity surged through me. A smile tugged on the corner of his lips as his hand lingered, continuing to send a current through me. "I'll meet you in the library after school."

I could only imagine the expression that was on my face as I responded with a nod. Once he rounded the corner, Julie was hysterical.

"Hello, Mr. Touchy Pants! You're so right, you guys *totally* have energy. I felt like I was watching the juiciest part of a movie just now! Tell me *everything*!"

I tried to compose myself. "I don't even know what to *say*, Jewls! I don't know what the hell that was." I felt the heat begin to radiate off my face. I was probably as red as a tomato.

"Well, what happened?"

"Nothing! The whole time we were working on the project."

Julie was disgruntled with that information. "What! No little chit-chats? Flirtatious looks? Suggestive innuendos?"

"*Nada*, it was all work. Then we get back here and I thought it was just me, but that was totally something just now, wasn't it?"

Julie shrieked in excitement. "Totally!"

I couldn't hide it, I was freaking out just as much as she was. My cheeks hurt from smiling so hard. "What do I do?"

"Invite him to your party! *Duh!*"

"I'm gonna do it!"

We both started screaming and jumping up and down until we realized where we were and all the looks we were getting from people in the hall. Embarrassed, we couldn't stop laughing as we grabbed our books, locked arms and headed to our next class.

* * * * *

It seemed as though time couldn't go by fast enough. I swore the clock had been set on 2:45pm forever! Only twenty minutes left until school was over. I was trying to play it out in my mind exactly how I should go about inviting him to the party without making it obvious how much I actually wanted him there. Adrenaline had taken over me now, my previous feelings of fatigue a distant memory, and restlessness had taken its place. Something about him screamed out for me to keep my distance, but the other part longed to know more about him.

When the bell finally rang, I bolted out of the classroom like a bat out of hell. Once at my locker, I did a quick once-over in the mirror. My hair was decent; nothing in my teeth, and my cappuccino skin had a rosy glow to it. Not too shab if I said so myself. I freshened up with a little spritz of spray, a stick of gum and a little lipgloss, then hurried over to the library.

The same table we occupied throughout lunch was empty, so I settled in there to wait. I figured now would be a good time to text Mom reminding her that I would be late tonight. Knowing her she would be waiting out front for me to make sure I didn't have to take the bus. As I was flipping through our notes, my "Zander Alert" went off. Just on time. I looked up smiling, expecting to see him, but no one was there. I scanned the library, but couldn't spot him.

"Huh." I spoke aloud to myself. "I could've sworn ..."

I shrugged my shoulders and returned to reviewing the notes. Suddenly, the air crackled around me with a current of static that gave me goose bumps. I started to feel uneasy and turned to glance behind me. Nothing. When I turned back to face the table, I gasped and nearly jumped out of my chair.

"Hey."

I couldn't believe my eyes. Zander was sitting across from me. "How did you do that?" I yelled, mystified.

He laughed out loud. "I told you I have a few tricks of my own." He was so pleased with himself, his laugh was infectious, and as stunned as I was, I couldn't help but smile back.

"You almost gave me a heart attack! I didn't even hear you come in." He was still laughing. "You should've seen your face! Priceless!"

I caught myself staring. He always came across so mysterious or intense, so seeing him this carefree was a treat. He continued to chuckle to himself as he put his notes on the table.

"I had a chance to get the rest of the information we needed last period."

I looked down at the papers. "Oh. So I guess we're finished?"

"Yeah, I guess we are." He crossed his arms, content.

I tried to conceal my disappointment. "Well, I guess I should tell my mom to come get me earlier then, since we won't need the extra hour anymore."

"Actually," he leaned forward, resting his chin on his palms, "I thought we could just hang out." His auburn eyes locked on me in such a way that it made me feel as though butterflies were fluttering recklessly in my stomach.

My palms started to get sweaty. Inside I was overjoyed, but terrified at the same time. I had to keep my composure cool. I shrugged my shoulders lightly. "OK, yeah. Cool."

"Are you feeling any better? You seemed really out of it this morning."

It seemed like our exchange this morning was days ago. I had completely engulfed myself in how I would invite him to the party that I practically forgot my previous feelings of crappiness earlier. "Yeah, I haven't been sleeping great these past couple nights."

His eyes pierced into mine. "Why?"

How does one respond to that exactly? I thought. *Gee, Zander, turns out I'm actually losing my mind. Nightmares, hallucinations, the whole sha-bang!* That would for sure send him running for the hills.

"I think I'm just stressing too much."

"About what?" *He was quite the curious George, wasn't he?* I observed. Although, his curiosity gave me the perfect opening I'd been waiting for. *Here goes nothing.*

"I'm having a party for my birthday. I don't usually throw parties, but my mom and Jewls have pretty much planned the entire thing. Back in my parents' village turning seventeen is supposedly a big deal."

"Really?" He leaned in closer.

"Yeah, it's basically when a child crosses over to become an adult, blah, blah blah." I hadn't realized I'd begun to twiddle my thumbs, keeping my gaze locked on them. "But um ... you should uh ... come. You know," I added hastily, "if - if you're not doing anything June first."

I could feel the red sink into my face. That was not the casual delivery I had planned. I peeked up at him through my lashes. His expression was hard to describe. It appeared as if he was having an internal war with himself until he locked eyes with me.

"I'd love to."

I gave him a coy smile. "Great." The trumpets sounded off a triumphant melody in my head.

"So, any progress with your parents?"

"Progress?"

"Yeah, you, well ... *Julie* mentioned you were having a hard time with them keeping things from you? Any luck?"

"Oh, no, not really. I mean, I think I was just being dramatic." There was *no way* I was coming clean to Zander.

The natural glow in his eyes dulled. "Oh?"

An uneasy feeling started to form in the pit of my stomach. Why do I feel like I just upset him?

"I mean, they were hiding stuff yeah, but they told me it's nothing that I should be worried about, so I just let it go." A current began to thrum against my skin.

"Do you believe that?" He raised an eyebrow.

Was he mocking me? I stared dumbfounded. "They're my parents. Of course I believe them."

The reality was that this was the first time in my life that I've ever felt wronged by them. Dad was trying. I know it kills him to keep things from me. But Mom, she was going above and beyond to keep me in the dark. Little did she know, the dark is the last place I should be.

The static began to thrum more intensely, sending sharp currents through me. The sensation made me wince. Something was happening to me. Something bad. Not another episode! I had to get out of here before Zander thought I was crazy. I had to breathe.

"Would you excuse me for a second?"

Before he could respond, I was out of my seat, bolting to the bathroom. My whole body began to shake violently with electricity. I lunged for the sink to support my weight, gasping. Multiple images flashed in my head of lion-like creatures, green flashing lights and what looked like a little girl with wings. I closed my eyes as hard as I could trying to banish the visions that kept springing forward. So many voices were in my head at once, it was hard to decipher one from the other. I slammed my hands over my ears.

"STOP!"

Pleading wouldn't help me now. My body continued to shake. I fell to the floor in a fetal position. Tears began flowing out of the corners of my closed eyes. Dizziness disabled me. Was I going to die here? My skin was on fire, burning me from the inside out, every fibre of my body was consumed by this incredible heat, torturing me. I wanted to scream, but the crippling pain kept my teeth locked together as I started to convulse. The swelter of the continuous electricity that surged through me was unbearable.

Finally, a coolness began to soothe my skin. My convulsions slowly began to cease. The cooling sensation slowly trickled down from the top of my head to my feet. My heart rate began to slow, the scorching subsided, and the current became a light tingle. All the voices stopped, except for one.

This low angelic voice that called out my name. I slowly opened my eyes, my vision blinded by tears.

Despite my blurred vision, there was one distinct thing I was extremely aware of in that moment. The silhouette of the man from my nightmares was staring down at me.

Chapter 6: Fate

I laid there, limp. Defeated. This was it.

The figure bent down and I flinched away, holding my hand up as a shield. That's when I felt his cool hands slowly lower mine and tilt my chin up.

"Angel, can you hear me?" The voice was like an echo.

His hands lightly brushed the damp hair off my forehead and wiped the tears from my cheeks. My vision started to clear and the silhouette came into form. It was Zander.

His hair fell in his face, his eyes full of concern as he cupped my face in his hands. His hands were so cool, as if he'd just come inside from a cold day without gloves. They felt like silk against my skin, calming and cooling it down with their gentle touch.

Disoriented, my voice came out as a whimper. "Zander?"

"Angel, are you alright?" His tone was gentle, but pained.

I felt his arms twine around me, lifting me up to my feet. My head was spinning. Searching for balance, I held onto his solid arms for support. His whole body was so cool. Without realizing, I leaned into him, resting my head on his shoulder, breathing in his scent and basking in the refreshing cool that continued to soothe my ignited skin. He stiffened for a moment, but exhaled and wrapped one arm around me. I would be mortified at myself if I wasn't so dizzy. The coolness of his body revitalized me like a splash of cold water. I felt a safeness being in his arms that filled me with a warmth I've never experienced before. The weight of the burdens that haunted and tortured me were gone in his embrace. He was my anchor, grounding me with perfect balance. I couldn't stop the sobs that now escaped me.

He began to lightly rub my back. "Shhhhh, it's OK. You're OK."

I tilted my chin up to face him, locked in his stare. Time froze. We stared into each other's eyes without saying a word. He reached up and brushed another tear from my cheek. A new warmth spread through me, tickling all my senses. He slowly bent forward and I closed my eyes, anticipating the touch of his lips.

The bathroom door flew open. Mrs. Thachet, the librarian, appraised us with a stunned expression.

"What's going on in here?" she shrieked. "This is completely inappropriate!"

I pulled away quickly, wiping my face. Talk about embarrassing. Zander countered Mrs. Thachet quickly, concern filling his voice.

"Please excuse us, Mrs. Thachet, but I heard screaming and came in here to find Angel visibly upset."

Her steely enraged eyes became soft and understanding. "I heard screams too. Angel, are you alright? What happened?" She reached out and placed her hand on my shoulder.

"Yeah, I'm sorry, I uh …" I had no idea what to say. My mind went blank.

"She has really bad migraines, they're crippling. She wasn't feeling too well back in the library, so I wanted to make sure she was alright. My mother also gets really bad migraines, so I knew what to do." Zander chimed in.

My mouth hung open, perplexed. Why was he lying for me?

"Oh, you poor thing." Mrs. Thachet put her arms around my shoulders. "Come on, dear, let's get you to the nurse." She looked up to Zander and praised. "Thank you so much Zander for helping her."

He humbly smiled back. "I'm happy to help. I'll see that she gets to the nurse, it's not a problem."

"Oh, perfect." She handed me back over to him. "Take your time, sweetie."

I half-smiled back, embarrassed, giving her a grateful nod.

We all exited the bathroom. Zander quickly went to get our things, and waved good-bye to Mrs. Thachet as we began to walk down the hallway. When we were safely out of sight from the library, I turned to Zander, crossing my arms defensively.

"Why did you do that?"

He folded his arms in the same manner. "Well, I figured you wouldn't want to tell the librarian that you've been having cryptic visions."

My heart felt like it dropped on the floor. I felt the color drain out of my face. "What did you say?"

He stared hard at me. "You heard what I said."

I stiffened. "I don't know what you're talking about."

"Really? So...last night, you weren't told in your dream that someone was coming for you? And, let me guess, you haven't been seeing strange creatures either?" He smiled matter of factly. "Sound familiar?"

I opened my mouth to speak, but no words came out. Damn Julie! I cursed. I can't believe she told him everything. How could she? She's supposed to be my best friend. I was furious. I finally responded to him in a scathing tone, "Frankly, it's none of your business."

I felt the tears begin to prick my eyes. The betrayal stung. I turned on my heels and began walking in the other direction. In an instant, Zander was in front of me. I gasped, frozen in disbelief.

"It wasn't Julie." His eyes penetrated mine.

"How did you do that?" My voice trembled. That wasn't a trick. That was real. He moved so fast - *too fast* to be human.

"You want answers, right?"

I stared blankly at him, still shaken. He grabbed me by my arms firmly.

"Angel, listen to me," he wasn't quite yelling, but his tone was aggressive enough to make me wince. "Meet me at midnight tonight at the park outside your house. Come alone and don't tell anyone. Not Julie, and definitely not your parents."

I felt a lonely tear trickle down my cheek. "Why should I trust you? How do I know you're not going to hurt me?"

A deadly grin formed on his lips. "Believe me, if I wanted to hurt you, I wouldn't need to meet with you for an ambush. I could've taken you out anytime I wanted." He loosened his grip on my arms, eyes darkening with truth. He wasn't bluffing.

Once he let go, I debated running, but with his speed he would catch me for sure. Then an idea formed in my head. All I had to do was execute it. I was a black belt in karate. Mom said it would be useful to know how to protect myself, and I've never had to until now. I planned to knock him out cold and make a run for it. Knowing my mother, she was more than likely early, already waiting for me.

I closed my eyes and sighed. "OK."

His returning smile assured me he wouldn't see this one coming. I began to center myself, taking in a deep breath. I flexed my hands at my sides and in one swift motion, slammed my palm as hard as I could into his beautiful face. The sound of his body hitting the ground was all the confirmation I needed to start running.

I ran as fast as I could down the hallway. My lungs felt like they were on fire, but I kept running. I rounded the corner and could see the double doors that lead to the front main hallway. Almost there.

Faster than my foot could hit the ground, I was down. Pinned to the floor with Zander on top of me. His eyes were no longer the auburn I'd grown to adore. They glowed a bright red. Horrified, my scream was muffled by his hands covering my mouth.

"Bad idea," he hissed. He grinned deviously to reveal his sharp fangs. "I give you an inch and you take a mile."

I thrashed underneath him, desperate to break free.

"Oh, c'mon, Angel! Don't act like I'm the only monster in this hallway." With lightning speed, he grabbed the mirror out of my backpack and held it up to my face.

This was worse than any of my nightmares. My eyes were a bright golden yellow with a small black pupil, identical to those of a lion with wide irises filling up all the white space. The corners on each side were black, emphasizing its new yellow color. He tilted the mirror slightly back and forth and my eyes glowed a silvery blue-green, like a cat's in the dark. I stopped thrashing and stared at myself, stunned.

"Ready to behave?"

My mind reeled with the abomination that stared back at me. Zander was right. I was a monster. I felt a heavy lump build up in my throat. I was so overwhelmed. What am I? What was he? He said he had answers for me, and as much as everything told me not to trust him, he was the only one that I had to trust if I ever wanted to find out the truth. I nodded my head in agreement.

"Good girl." Every word seemed to be laced with ice. "Now listen. If you try anything like that stunt you just pulled again, I will paralyze you. One bite and you won't be able to move for hours. Understand?" I stared, bewildered. "I'm going to let go of you now. I highly suggest you cooperate." His eyes slowly dulled back to their auburn colour, his fangs retracting.

Slowly, he lifted his hand off my mouth. He must've seen the defeat in my demeanour as he lifted himself off me, his eyes becoming softer. Once he was upright, he held out his hand to help me up. I stared at it hesitantly.

"I'm not going to hurt you." His eyes were warm and honest. My trembling hands reached out for his. "That a girl."

I couldn't help but stare at him. I was flabbergasted. So many questions rushed into my mind. I watched as he picked up my backpack and collected everything that had flown out, handing it back to me with an awkward smile.

I felt my chin begin to tremble and the lump in my throat become thicker. "Am I really a monster?"

I couldn't tell if it was pity or sadness in his eyes as he let out a sigh. "I know nothing makes sense to you right now, but it will. I promise."

"So, what now?" My voice still sounded shaky.

He let out another more exasperated sigh. "You go home and act normal. Your parents can't find out that you know what's going on, or that you know about me. It will just put everyone in more danger. Your mom seemed to feel my presence yesterday, which is a bad sign. For me, that is."

The memory of her in the car after school came back. It was Zander after all that had made her act like that. "Why?"

"If your parents had any idea that I was going to this high school, or that I was anywhere near you, they would take you and disappear. A long time ago, I was someone else. I've done unforgivable things." He looked tormented by his thoughts. "But that was in the past. I want to help keep you safe, and I can't do that if I don't know where you are."

I was so confused. "Keep me safe? From who? That woman? Who is she?"

"Like I said, I'll explain everything tonight. You have to find a way to get out of the house."

"How do you even know where I live?" It seemed like a frivolous question in spite of all the craziness, but it still made me curious.

He was growing impatient. "Enough with the hundred and one questions. Your mom has been outside for the past five minutes. Just do whatever is necessary tonight to get out."

"How do you know my mom's here?"

Pinching the bridge of his nose, his words came out in a rush as if to shut me up. "Because! The same way you can sense me, I can sense you. OK? That goes for your parents as well. There. Happy? Now go."

I felt my mouth hanging open. "You knew this whole time that I could sense you?"

He crossed his arms and stared, clearly not impressed. I wanted to pinch myself, but there was no use. This was actually happening. Every last awful, horrible bit of it. I put on my backpack and started for the doors until realization dawned on me.

"Wait!" I spun back to face Zander. "My eyes! I can't go see my mom looking like a freak! She'll know."

He rolled his eyes. "Your eyes are fine."

I quickly pulled off my backpack and grabbed my mirror to check for myself. They were their usual hazel and gold colour. I deflated in relief. "How did they do that?"

"You don't listen, do you?" He stared for a moment, mouth locked in a hard line. "You were upset."

I raised my eyebrows skeptically, "But I've been upset before and that's never happened."

"Never that upset." He rubbed his jaw.

He was right. Damn it.

I turned back around to head outside when Zander called out in an arrogant tone, "What? A hundred and one questions and no goodbye?"

Was he for real? I continued stomping away.

As I entered the main hallway, I could see Mom's car waiting outside through the tall windows. I took in a deep breath, trying as best as I could to compose myself. Mom instantly picked up on my vibe once I got in the car.

"What's the matter, sweetie?" She put her hands on top of my head, like one would a child.

I gave her the best fake smile I could and complained that I wasn't feeling well. She seemed to buy it, telling me she'll make me her famous soup for dinner that will have me feeling like a champ. Thankfully, the rest of the way home she gave me my space.

I zoned out, recalling everything that happened. I went from practically being obsessed with Zander, to almost kissing him, to finding out he's, excuse me … *that we're* something other than human. Along with the lovely fact that he is the key to all the missing pieces of the puzzle I've been so desperate to figure out. My head felt like it was spinning again. Last week my biggest worry was what to wear and now my life had been completely derailed. Anger began to take over. How could my parents do this? How could they keep such a significant fact that we're *beasts* from me? Did they honestly think I would never find out? All these unnecessary secrets and lies to supposedly protect me? I don't buy it for a second! They are so selfish! Did they not think of how I would feel? What it would do to me to know that they could have prevented all this turmoil I've been going through the past couple days by simply coming clean!

I knew deep down I was being irrational, but I didn't care. This was their fault. Everyone has a choice, and they chose to lie to me. Now I'm stuck depending on the most gorgeous man I've ever seen to be the one to let me in on the scoop. Here I was thinking he actually liked me…but then what was that in the bathroom earlier? He was so gentle with me, so tender, so deliciously close. The memory warmed me. He was totally going to kiss me. I smiled to myself, feeling the heat spread on my cheeks, remembering how amazing it felt to be locked in his arms, pressed up against his cool skin –

"Angel? We're home, honey. Aren't you going to get out?" Mom yelled through the car window, snapping me out of my haze.

I embarrassingly chuckled to myself, undoing my seatbelt.

I got through the entire night being as cool as a cucumber. Careful of my expressions and keeping myself guarded from my parents. After Mom's infamous soup, I retreated to my room and threw myself down on the bed. I was exhausted, craving for a quick nap but I knew better to think that I would actually have a relaxed rest. A soft knock sounded at my door.

"Hey, sweetie. Got a minute for me?" Dad said, poking his head in.

No! No I do not have a minute for you! I wanted to scream at him, but kept it mellow. "What's up?"

He closed the door behind him and came to sit on the edge of my bed, making sure to keep his voice low. "I wanted to talk about last night."

I had to keep my face nonchalant, but I could hear the bitterness come through in my voice. "What about it?"

"I know you've been feeling left out. That's why you were outside trying to listen, right?" He leaned forward to put his hand gently over mine.

I narrowed my eyes. "Dad, honestly, my head's hurting and I had a really crappy day, so I'm in no mood to talk about your theories. Can you just leave me alone, please?" I had to find a way to make sure my parents would leave me alone tonight. Therefore, Operation Jerk was in full effect.

"OK, sweetie. Do you want me to get you anything?"

"No." I snapped.

I watched as my dad slowly exited my room, heavy-hearted. Good, I thought viciously. I glanced over at the clock. 7:45pm. I still had another four hours until my grand escape.

A text came through on my phone from Julie.

How'd it go?

If only she knew. I wanted to tell her everything, especially about the almost-kiss. How much of a hypocrite am I to be upset at my parents for not telling me the truth and here I was about to lie to my best friend.

Fine. We finished the project.

Ya ya that's great, anything juicy happen?

Nope. All work.

Ugh! Really?

Yup.

KK well, c u 2morrow, we'll devise a plan to get some action going on.

LOL! K. Night.

Night.

I exhaled resting my phone on the side table. There would be action alright. I had no idea what I would be stepping into tonight, but I did know for certain that everything was going to change.

★ ★ ★ ★ ★

The hours passed by incredibly slow. Mom came in to say a quick goodnight some time after 10:00pm. I'm sure Dad had let her know about the mood I was in and to leave me be. I was fighting sleep, my eyes stung every time I blinked. I must have splashed cold water on my face ten times just to keep them open. When my clock finally read 11:45pm I peeked out my door to my parents room. Soft snores echoed in the hallway. It was time.

I impressed myself with my stealth. Last night I was so emotional, sounding like a cow banging down the stairs thus alerting my dad, who happens to be a very light sleeper, that I was up to something. Tonight I made sure not to make a sound. Once outside, adrenaline kicked in, giving me the boost I needed to start jogging to the park. Thankfully the park was only a seven-minute run. Regardless of the short distance I was out of breath. Being sleep-deprived made everything feel like it took the strength of an army, completely draining me. I bent over, resting my hands on my knees to catch my breath and looked at the time. 11:58pm.

"On time. I like that." Zander's voice sounded from the darkness.

Startled, I jolted back to standing upright. I looked around, but couldn't spot him anywhere.

"Where are you?"

A low chuckle came from the bushes behind me followed by a rustling. I spun around quickly to face the disturbance. Two bright glowing red orbs shone from the bushes back at me. I was frozen in shock. Zander appeared from out of the undergrowth, approaching me with a slowness that was definitely predatory, his eyes losing their glow completely once he was in sight.

His mouth formed into a slow grin. "So glad you could make it."

"What are you?" My heart felt like it would pound right out of my chest.

He walked over casually to sit on the bench, smiling obsequiously. "I'm an Obiri. Although, on Earth, my kind are referred to as vampires."

Did he seriously just say vampire? I tried to collect myself and stop my eyes from bulging. I knew coming here I would find out things I couldn't possibly begin to understand. There was no turning back now.

"If you're a vampire, how were you in the sun yesterday? Don't you like, go up in flames or something?"

He choked back a laugh. "No, that's myth. The sun simply irritates my eyes. With a pair of shades I can manage just fine."

Interesting. "What did you mean when you said *on Earth*? You're from another planet?"

He laughed to himself and patted the empty spot next to him on the bench. "Galaxy, but yes. Please have a seat, we may be here for a while."

"I'll stand, thanks."

"I won't bite." He was definitely amused with himself. He patted the spot again. I hesitated. "I can go if you like. Leave you to figure it all out on your own." He began to rise.

"NO!" I groaned. "OK, OK!" I started my slow walk towards him. The seat felt like ice underneath me. "You better not try anything," I warned.

He threw his head back and laughed. "I believe I should be the one telling you that. If I remember correctly, you attacked me first."

"I did not! You were grabbing me, that's called assault."

"If you would have taken the time to listen instead of acting like such a human, I wouldn't have had to take matters into my own hands."

I crossed my arms, offended. "What's that supposed to mean? 'Acting like such a human' You were scaring me!"

"No. *You* were being a brat stomping off in a hissy fit."

I glared at him, and he at me. This was going to be a long night. I drew out an exasperated breath. "I didn't come here for you to criticize me. You said you have answers."

"Correct."

I waited. He just stared expectantly. "Umm, anytime now."

He pressed his mouth in a hard line. "I cannot give answers without *questions*, genius."

I narrowed my eyes at him, speaking every word with vehemence. "Fine. What. Am. I?"

"Ah, progress! You're an Oleah."

"Which is..."

"You're more cat than anything else. Lion to be specific. To give you a better idea, you're like a centaur in your true form, however instead of the other half being a horse, it's a lion. You stand upright on your back legs and have the ability to morph into a lion, which is how your kind hunts. The Oleahs have extremely heightened senses that are connected with the environment. Your temperature becomes altered as a warning of danger or of anyone from Kindren. Your kind are impressive hunters and known throughout the galaxies for your agility, speed and loyalty."

I stopped breathing.

"Angel?"

I shook myself out of it. *That might explain the "Zander Alerts"*, I thought. I needed to know more.

"What's Kindren?"

"Kindren is a planet where all beings of darkness dwell. Every evil creature or monster that humans on Earth can think of reside there. It is ruled by Sindrell, Lucifer's sister, the most powerful sorceress in all the galaxies."

"Lucifer? Like Satan?"

"That is another name for him, yes."

My mouth went dry. I stood up involuntarily. Astounded.

Zander reached up and gently grabbed my hands, pulling me back down. "Still with me?"

"I - I - I think so." I eyed him cautiously. "Are you from Kindren?"

"I lived there yes, but not originally. Vampires were created here on Earth. Do you know the story of Adam and Eve?"

I nodded, too overwhelmed to speak.

"Perfect. God had given them free reign in the Garden of Eden with only one rule. When Eve broke that rule, that was the world's first sin. She had allowed impurity into her life. After she and Adam were cast out, it was the first time they ever experienced grief, pain and hunger. Cursed to live a life of trials and tribulations because they had sinned. Eve became sickly from disease and famine. She was consumed with bitterness and hate for the punishment her and Adam had to endure. On her death bed, Eve struck a deal with Satan, thinking that she would have a second chance at life. She should have learned her lesson from the first time that he could not be trusted. Her corpse rose from her grave without a heartbeat and an uncontrollable hunger for blood, which was the only thing that made her feel again. She fed on humans hoping to regain her soul, infecting every victim with her venomous bite.

"For centuries vampires resided on Earth, evolving and multiplying until the humans started to fight back. That's when Sindrell intervened, offering vampires a chance to live without the fear of being burned or staked on a new planet she created called Kindren. It was a refuge for all creatures that were either being cast out or killed off because of the damage they had caused on their own planets."

"How did they feed?" I was engulfed by the overload of information.

"Every planet in each galaxy has portals. The portals were created to transport the leaders of each planet to meet with each other for affirmation of peace throughout the galaxies. You see, when God cast out Satan from heaven, he allowed the other angels a chance to create their own galaxies and govern them. Satan was jealous and decided to do the same with his only sister who chose by her own will to leave heaven to be with her brother. Where there was good, evil was not too far behind. So when Sindrell created Kindren, she made sure every creature would have access to their planets of origin to either feed or seek revenge."

"If I'm a *monster* ..." The word sounded like acid on my tongue, "... how come Oleah's are not from Kindren?"

He narrowed his eyes. "So typical that you would deem anything nonhuman as a monster. The Oleah species were created by one of the angels. Your planet, Uforika, was created as a jungle paradise. Over the years many angels and cherubs from heaven immigrated there permanently. It was the most beautiful planet ever created, blessed by God." His expression changed. He looked grief-stricken.

"*Was?*" I repeated. "As in not anymore?"

"No." He looked down as if he was ashamed.

I wanted to reach out and console him. "What happened to it?"

He sighed. "Sindrell became obsessed with power. She resented that the angels had so many planets and she only one. She wanted to rule them all. She conspired with Satan on combining their darkness to take over and force each planet into submission. They set out invading each planet, taking out the leaders by sucking out their power. Once the leaders were destroyed, she made the inhabitants pledge their lives to her. One by one she destroyed and took over each planet. Until only one remained: Uforika.

"She knew that Uforika was the most protected planet, cherished by God. Satan refused to go with her, knowing that although their combined powers were great, they still did not have enough to face the angels. She felt betrayed by his cowardice, which only fuelled her new unlimited powers. She picked out the most ruthless killers from Kindren to help her invade the planet." His eyes burned into mine with agony. "I was one of them."

He continued, no longer looking at me.

"When I fled to Kindren back in the 1500s, I was full of hate. The humans had killed my mother. You see, we were different than the others. We evolved. Only hunting when we needed to feed, and not by the thirst to be superior. We never killed anyone, we always kept the humans alive by tricking them into allowing us to feed from them and then erasing the memory from their thoughts so they would never know what happened. It sounds awful, but we were civilized. Other vampires scorned us for wanting to live amongst humans and be treated like one ourselves. They tricked a human into thinking we were vicious killers that had to be eliminated." His eyes began to glow bright red. "I'll never forget her screams. I was in town getting water from the well. I heard the crowd, but never thought they would be coming for us. I realized they were at my house by her screams. I ran as fast as I could, but I couldn't get to her in time. The fire had already spread." He got up and began to pace in front of me, anguished by his memories.

His hands balled into tight fists as he growled; the low rippling sound sending a cold current shuddering through me. Enraged, he punched the tree beside us, shattering it in half. Breathing heavily, he ran his fingers through his now wild dark hair. He began again, sounding pained, but more composed.

"Sindrell found me that night. My hate and pain had been so strong it drew her to me. She told me about Kindren and I left with her. She was my saviour. Living on Kindren changed me. Being around so many dark forces drew out the monster that hibernated within. I allowed the hate I felt to kill my sense of reason. I was possessed by it, and wanted revenge. Every time I visited Earth was to kill. I massacred innocent families thinking it would help settle the score of the emptiness I felt inside. Sindrell praised me, making me her second in command, telling me that no one had as much fight in them as I did. For years I wanted to please her, make her proud of me, thinking that her presence and views of me could substitute not having my mother. When she revealed to me her plan to take over Uforika, I was all for it. I didn't know beauty or happiness anymore and didn't want there to be any of it, anywhere. The day before we planned our attack, word came in from Satan that Uforika had something that Sindrell wanted more than anything: *you*."

"Me?" I choked out, feeling like all the air had been knocked out of me. "Why?"

Zander's eyes faded back to normal as he began to walk slowly towards me, his expression deadly.

"Your parents were the leaders of Uforika. Their hearts were pure. Everything they did, every act to improve the planet and its kind, was out of pure love. This love was rare, only the angels in heaven possessed it. They were tempted to become more powerful and corrupt, but refused, not wanting to be superior, but equal. It was unheard of and because of their selflessness, God crowned them king and queen of that galaxy so that each planet in their orbit would strive to be like the Oleahs. Sindrell was maddened with jealousy because of it. When the king and queen had you, God blessed your mother's womb with an unlimited amount of power that could be used to destroy any enemy. You were born indestructible."

I stood up again involuntarily, mouth wide open. He continued towards me until he was an arm's length away.

"Satan caught wind of this and told Sindrell. With your indestructibility she would have the power she so desperately craved to be able to go up against heaven. So we set out for Uforika, looking for you with the goal to rob you of your powers and destroy you. The cherubs alerted the angels and closed all the portals in every galaxy. They are the only beings that have the power to do so. They hid you and your parents by sending you to Earth to live as humans. Only the wing glitter of one cherub could reopen the portal back to Earth: Coral.

"We invaded Uforika. The Oleahs were no use to us. They would never submit knowing that their monarchy was safe. They rebelled against us. It was the biggest war in all the galaxies. We were outnumbered and forced to retreat back to Kindren. You see, without you, Sindrell will always be a step behind from her ultimate take-over."

I blinked uncontrollably, stunned. I couldn't believe what I was hearing. I was indestructible, and a *princess*? My parents were the king and queen of an entire galaxy and Zander was the right-hand man to the devil's sister, responsible for ruining the place my parents loved so much? My head was spinning. I put my palm over my forehead and began walking. I needed a minute to digest everything. I took in deep breaths, but realized this story wasn't over. There was more to it. I spun back around to face him.

"If the portal to Earth was blocked, how did you get here?"

"Sindrell drew up a potion that almost matched a cherub's wing glitter. All she needed was one feather from Coral's wings to test it. The powers that she possesses are incredible, she could find access to just about any closed door. She managed to unlock the portal back to Uforika and sent me to collect it. Cherubs shed their feathers regularly and keep them for healing remedies. I snuck into her chambers and took a feather from her stash. When I returned to Kindren, Sindrell used up so much of her power that she wasn't strong enough to go through the portal herself, so she sent me here."

"To kill me." I crossed my arms, tears stinging my vision.

"No. To bring you back with me to Kindren." He stood there, so nonchalant after what he'd just said.

"Oh, excuse me, for HER to kill me!" I felt the hot tears trickle down my face.

"Yes."

"*Why* are you telling me all this? Did you think I would really just *go* with you because you decided to give me a history lesson?"

He stood there blankly. "No."

"Then what? Why are you pretending to help me?" I wasn't about to go down that easily. I quickly wiped my tears and put my arms up, ready to fight. He might be fast, but I knocked him flat once and I could do it again.

He raised his hands in submission. "Whoa! Hey! Easy! I'm not pretending, I want to help you."

"WHY?"

"Because Sindrell isn't enough for me," he yelled. "I wanted *so* badly for her to love me like my mother did, but she *never will.* She doesn't care about me, the lust she has for power is the only thing that has ever mattered to her. I see that now. Besides, when I'm around you I feel ... different." He lowered his eyes as if he were embarrassed.

I slowly dropped my arms. I felt so conflicted. I was deeply attracted to him and part of me didn't care what he'd done in the past, he wasn't the same now. But the other part felt like I'd be betraying not only my family, but my *people* if I trusted him. What if this was all an act and he was still the monster he claimed he no longer was?

His eyes found me again and I couldn't move. I was fixed in place, bewitched by the magnetic energy that was so thick between us, wanting nothing more than to be closer to him.

"How do I know I can trust you?" I whispered.

He deflated, letting out a deep breath, closing his eyes. "Do you believe in fate, Angel?"

I studied his perfect face. "Should I?"

"I believe that fate brought me here to you." He opened his eyes and they burned into mine with such intensity I felt as though my knees were about to give way underneath me.

"I've been here for five years looking for you, searching every country and every school for the girl with the lion eyes." His lips twitched with a smile. "Being around humans, I felt something changing in me, but it was so alien I couldn't recognize it. The first couple weeks it was an act, pretending to be a human student, forcing myself to communicate with humans again to search for you. After a couple months I realized what was changing in me. I was regaining my sense of reason, my soul. I found myself enjoying communicating with humans, enjoying Earth and all it has to offer. Music, art, language, friendship, compassion, love.

"I would check in with Sindrell at first once every other day, then once a week and as more time passed, once every two months. But when I finally found you, I wasn't sure at first until I witnessed first-hand how your senses reacted and when our eyes met. I knew. Yet I couldn't bring myself to tell her."

He closed the gap between us. "You intrigued me. You were so shy, so fragile, so ... happily and unknowingly human. I followed you home that night and heard your parents on the porch with Coral."

I pulled away from him, stung by his confession. Little lines creased his forehead as his eyebrows drew together. He looked down to hide his disappointment.

"I'm not too sure what Coral said. I didn't even know who they were talking to, to be honest with you, until you mentioned Coral's name and I realized then that they were communicating telepathically. The only thing I knew for sure in that moment was that they knew I was here. They became so helpless and vulnerable. I saw how much they loved you and wanted to protect you. Believe it or not, it touched me, and I realized then that I too wanted to protect you."

"They wanted to protect me by lying to me. By keeping secrets from me!" I countered.

"They don't know what's been happening to you. At lunch yesterday when I asked, I didn't know you too had overheard. I thought you were lying about not knowing anything and that your parents had told you. I had to be sure."

"Well, what *is* happening to me? Why am I having all these nightmares and visions?" I was yelling again.

"You only have access to some of your powers once danger from Kindren is near. I've been around you quite a bit these last couple days, so your senses have been on overdrive. Your nightmares are actually memories – your *parents'* memories – what they've seen and feared. As for last night, I tricked you into thinking you were dreaming when you saw me in the kitchen to relay a message."

I felt my blood boil. "YOU DID *WHAT*? THAT WAS *YOU*?" I felt the urge to slap him across the face, but contained myself.

All the silhouettes in my dreams were of him! If they were in fact memories or fears that meant my parents feared him. How could I allow myself to fall for him when he's done so much wrong? This whole thing was wrong.

"Easy with the eye show," he warned. "You have to learn to control your temper. Every time you get upset, you tap into your true Oleah self, which is what Sindrell is watching for. Your incident in the bathroom today alerted her of your presence. She knows that I found you and she's been trying to contact me to find out your location, but I shut her out. She's close, *very* close. The minute she finds her way to Earth, she'll know where to find you, so please calm down."

He reached out for me, but I pulled back as if he was on fire and would burn me with his touch. I could see the hurt in his eyes.

"So what now? What do I do?" I crossed my arms.

He stared, failing to conceal the hurt in his eyes, but answered as if he wasn't affected. "Continue on as if you don't know anything. Your mother reacted to my presence the other day. She knows I'm close. She's been circling the school and the surrounding neighbourhood during the daytime to try and spot me lurking around. It hasn't dawned on her that I would be a student. She doesn't know me as Zander, but as Red. If your parents find out about us, they'll alert Coral and it will cause more harm than good."

"Then why did you want to work on the project at my house?"

"I wanted to search for more clues, see how much they know. The plan was to tap into their minds and suggestively persuade them into leaving the house so that we could come in. I would have the chance to search, then I would make up a story to leave before they could get back."

He just had an answer to everything, didn't he?

"OK, let me get this straight." I cupped my forehead in aggravation. "I'm just supposed to look my parents in the face knowing that I'm an indestructible *princess* blessed by God from another *galaxy*, whom Satan's sister wants to *kill* and has sent *you*, Zander or excuse me 'Red', to *capture*?"

"Correct."

I began to laugh sarcastically. "Yeah, sure! *No problemo*! I'll just continue to be the walking dead since I don't sleep anymore, *thanks to you*." I gave him a round of applause.

He crossed his arms, unamused.

"If you think my parents are going to believe my act, you're wrong. They'll know something is up, become *waaaay* more protective, then show up at school one day and see *you*. BOOM! Game over."

Zander's tone was flat and icy. "Listen, unless you want to send your parents to an early grave, I suggest you follow the plan."

"Don't you *dare* threaten my parents!"

Who did he think he was? I raged. OK, I knew who he was, but he had some nerve!

He closed the distance between us. Eyes blazing furiously into mine, "I'm NOT threatening them! Haven't you been listening? If they find out about this, Sindrell will sense it. She'll kill them, then come after you!"

"Yeah, and you as her little *servant* will just watch as it all unfolds, right?"

"NO!" He growled.

"Liar!"

My anger took over and I rose my hand up to strike him, but he caught it just before it hit his cheek, gripping my wrist tightly. His eyes were enraged and wild. I glared back at him just as infuriated. Before my mind could register what was happening his lips crushed down on mine in a frenzy. His hands moved from my wrists, wrapping themselves around my waist pulling me in closer. I eagerly laced my fingers into his hair, my heart pounding so fast I felt as though my blood was on fire, spreading its heat through my veins. I tried to catch my breath as the kiss deepened, becoming more urgent. My head was spinning; my world had changed.

Everything I knew as reality was just a cover up. Zander was behind so much of it. He was truly evil in his so-called past life, and now here he was in this life, the hottest guy I'd ever seen, kissing me.

The thought troubled me enough to give me the strength I needed to push him back. "Stop."

He stood breathless, eyes still hungry, staring at me. "I'm sorry."

With everything screaming inside me to stay in his arms, I forced myself to back away, taking in a deep breath, trying to collect myself. "I need time to think."

He closed his eyes, taking in a deep breath himself. "I understand. You should get going."

I knew that deep down the right thing to do was leave, despite the pull I still felt trying to draw me back to him. Maybe fate did bring us together, but what happens to us now?

"Yeah," was all I managed to choke out.

"I'll walk you close enough back to your place. Last thing I want is for your parents to start having the dreams too." He gently took my hand up to his soft, cool lips, greeting my knuckles with a light kiss. "Forgive me. Let's go."

Chapter 7: Ordinary Girl

I made it back in without a hitch and was now left to truly digest everything that had come to light. Galaxies, heaven and hell, cherubs and angels, sorceresses, Oleahs, rulers, wars, portals, vampires … To say I was overwhelmed was an understatement. I thought of all the lies I was led to believe about the supposed tribe my parents had said they were from back in the villages outside of Africa. Dad's painting of the family of lions came to mind, and I couldn't help but wonder. Was that us? Maybe it wasn't all so far away from the truth after all. There were no rebels, but they were in fact forced to leave to protect me. They didn't flee to another country, they fled to a freakin' new planet to become a whole new species! All because of me. I felt broken. My parents were not selfish, *I* was. All I could think about was *myself*. I could only imagine the pain they had to endure going from superior beings to having all their powers ripped away from them to become ordinary humans.

Tears pricked my eyes. I could hear their faint snores from my room. I would never understand why or how they could love me that much, but a desire welled up inside me to do the best I could to protect them in return. I would under no circumstances jeopardize their safety. If that meant keeping my mouth shut and parading around like a regular sixteen-year-old girl without the weight of the world on her shoulders, then so be it. They've been putting on this show for me for years. It was my turn now.

Maybe it was best to just supress everything I had learned tonight. Ignorance was bliss right? But what was I supposed to do about Zander? Flashes of our kiss flooded back into my head. My first kiss, a full-fledged make-out session, with a *vampire*! And not just any vampire, the right-hand man to the most evil being in all of creation! I groaned in misery, burying my face in my pillows. How am I supposed to face him tomorrow? He was my only source for information, so cutting him off was not exactly an option. I needed him.

* * * * *

I stood in front of a set of large, ornately designed, mahogany double doors. On either side of the doors hung broad torches, standing behind a metal swirl designed bucket. I tugged on the huge gold lion-headed knob with both hands, opening the massive doors.

Inside was a gorgeous room filled with wild white and pale pink bulb-like flowers I'd never seen before. They were magnificent, sparkling from the light of the hundreds of white tea light candles spread out amongst the vast room. On the walls hung enchanted paintings of lion cubs. Each time you moved, so would the paintings. Lush green plants traced the corners of the room. In the middle was a huge white and gold panelled playpen.

At the bottom of the pen was what resembled pink cotton candy. There was a little cherub inside with long strawberry blond curls, wearing a blue satin robe. Her electric turquoise eyes shone like gems. She was laughing, running to the other end of the pen, her curls bouncing behind her. I took a few more steps to get a closer look inside the pen to see what was chasing her, but couldn't see anything. From under the pillows, a little white lion cub pounced out, startling the little cherub. Her white majestic wings fluttered out from behind her, lifting her into the air. She laughed even harder now.

"Close, Princess, but I win!"

The little lion cub transformed into an Oleah toddler and that's when I recognized the little heart-shaped face. It was me. I frowned, stomping my paw.

"No! Bad!" I huffed.

The cherub glided back down to the ground, giggling. "Come on, Princess, you know it was fair and square. Remember, you must stay humble when things do not go your way." She began tickling me.

I couldn't help but smile to myself watching the interaction.

Then the door swung open and my jaw dropped. It was Mom in her Oleah form. She was stunning. Her hair was the same: smooth, long and black with sandy blonde highlights and little shells intertwined in the little braids that framed the front of her face. She wore a shiny diamond-like crown that wrapped as a band around her head, tracing along her ears, and hung through the holes in them as a long string. She was dressed in a long satin V-neck ivory-coloured robe with bell sleeves and two long slits up the sides of her strong lion legs.

"OK, you two, time for bed."

We both whined and Mom crossed her arms. The cherub hugged me goodbye, then glided over to Mom, embracing her as well. She fit perfectly in Mom's arms like a little toddler.

"Goodnight, my queen."

"Goodnight, Coral."

Coral glided over to the doors, turned back to wave goodbye again, and fluttered away.

The scene shifted once she left. The room was now empty and trashed. Inside the playpen were two creatures. The first was a werewolf, ripping through the fluffy material at the bottom of the pen, searching. The other was what I could only describe as a demon: tall with shiny blood-red, lizard-like skin, large horns on either side of its head and a long black beak. It too was thrashing through the pen with its razor sharp claws. The sight alone terrified me.

The door burst open and Zander came in, eyes blazing red, his mouth stained with fresh blood and his fangs out. He wore a shiny black and silver breastplate with black tights and knee-high medieval boots. His expression was sinister, no short of deadly. I almost didn't recognize him. It was as if he was possessed. He looked to both creatures expectantly. They simply shook their heads no.

"Keep looking! Leave no corner untouched!" He growled in an infuriated rage, then stormed out.

★ ★ ★ ★ ★

I woke up startled, to Dad knocking on the door.

"Time to get up honey," he said cheerfully.

"Yeah, OK." I grumbled.

I realized I was trembling when I reached for my glass of water on the end table. *Just another day in the life of an ordinary teenage girl*, I thought.

When I managed to peel myself out of bed to get to the shower, I stared at my reflection in the mirror. My eyes were puffy and red, accompanied by dark circles under them to match.

"Mmm, attractive." I groaned.

I let the water pound down on me. At the temperature I had it set, my skin should've been scalded by now, but I felt cold. Numb. Images of Zander from the dream flashed in my mind, sending a shiver down my spine. I wished that the water could wash away everything with it on its journey down the drain, cleansing me of my thoughts and worries.

Mom banged on the door. "Angel, did you fall asleep in the shower? Come on, we're going to be late, hurry up!"

The rest of the morning I had to listen to Mom lecture me on staying up too late and how tired I looked, that I needed to take better care of myself and blah blah blah. It didn't upset me. I just took it in like everything else.

Once she dropped me off Julie practically jumped me, going on and on about Zander, the party and how much she hated her biology teacher. I felt like I was having an out-of-body experience. I was going through the motions, seeing everything in a new light, realizing that I'd taken so much for granted. My parents, Julie's stories, her giddy personality, and above all, having the freedom to just be ordinary.

"Have you heard anything I've said?" Julie huffed.

"Sorry, Jewls, I have a lot on my mind today." I leaned into my locker to hang up my jacket.

"Like what?" she asked, concerned.

"I have a history test today, I was up pretty late trying to study." *Let the lies begin*, I thought miserably.

"Ugh, history is the *worst*! I don't know how you deal in that class, I would've dropped out by now," she laughed, carefree.

English and history went by in a haze. As I dragged my feet on the way to Spanish, my Zander alert went off. I kept walking, knowing I would have to face him eventually. He did after all sit beside me next period. There was nowhere left to run. Unless ... I skipped the class. Now there's a thought! Mom would kill me if she found out, although she couldn't be mad if I played the sick card. Truth of the matter was I wasn't ready to face him yet. I would take the coward's way out until I had a better grasp on my feelings. The more I allowed myself to become attached to him, the harder the dreams were for me to witness.

He truly was someone else in my dreams, someone dark. The vision of him last night haunted me. His eyes were so cold and empty. If they had found me that night, he would've been the one to bring me to my death. I shuddered, goose bumps erupting on my skin. I can't do this. Not today. I turned on my heels and headed back to my locker. I knew he was close, but with all the students in the hallway, he would be stupid to use his speed to catch up to me. This was my only shot to make a break for it.

Once at my locker I called Mom on my cell. She picked up after the second ring.

"Hi sweetie, what's wrong?" I can't say for sure if she sounded panicked, but it was close enough.

"I'm not feeling good, Mom, I think it was the tacos I had after first period. I feel like I'm gonna throw up." I played up the sickness in my voice as best as I could. I needed her sympathy.

"Didn't I warn you about the food in the cafeteria? I told you it's no good! I have no idea why you always eat there." She exhaled. "I'll have your father pick you up shortly, OK?"

"Thanks, Mom." Checkmate! Operation Ditch was in full effect.

"In the meantime, see if the nurse can make you a tea from the staff room, it might settle your stomach."

"Yeah, OK."

The moment I hung up the phone, relief swept over me. Now I just needed to get to the front without being seen. It would probably take Dad about twenty minutes to get here, so that gave me enough time to bolt before Julie started wandering the halls to look for me. I collected all my things and started towards the front. Thankfully the hallways were still packed, giving me the chance to blend in and not be so easily noticed.

Once I settled in at the office, I knew I was safe. The nurse put me in one of the back rooms to lay down and wait until my dad showed up. She draped a hot cloth over my forehead and eyes, relaxing me completely. The heat of the cloth soothed and actually warmed me, taking away the chill that seemed to linger.

When I heard the door open, I knew Dad was here and I'd be on my way home back to my room where I could lay in my comfy, cozy bed and watch Maury for the rest of the day. I decided to go out with a bang and put on my last little show for the spectators. I groaned, putting my hand on my stomach and whining like a child.

"Is my dad here?"

"Playing hooky are we, Princess?" Zander's low voice was gentle with traces of amusement.

I quickly sat up straight, realizing that we were alone in the room together.

"How did you get in here?"

He smirked. "Wouldn't you like to know?"

I crossed my arms, irritated that he'd ruined my plans. "Yeah, actually, I would."

"Why are you skipping class?"

He had so much nerve. I thought angrily. "Umm, for your information, I'm not feeling well."

He rolled his eyes. "Oh *please*, save your antics for the humans. I'm not a fool. There's nothing wrong with you."

"Yeah? How would you know?" *He thinks he's so slick!*

"Because I would be able to smell it, especially when you're weak, and you smell pretty healthy to me." He narrowed his eyes at me suspiciously. "So why are you ditching?"

Ugh! Stupid beautiful vampire and his stupid senses! I guess that would explain how he knew to find me in the bathroom yesterday. I put the cloth back over my eyes; he would be less distracting this way. I wouldn't have to stare at his smooth creamy skin and how his navy blue shirt complimented it perfectly, or the way his slicked-back hair emphasized the perfectly symmetrical bone structure of his face. I would just pretend like he's just another average kid like the rest of us. I had to test my resolve with him. The last thing I needed was another reason for my head to hurt.

"Are you avoiding me or something?"

I chuckled to myself. It was such a human thing for him to say despite the spot-on accuracy.

"No, I just didn't want to be here today." *Because of you.*

"Because of me?" He sounded so vulnerable, taking the thought directly out of my head.

I lowered the cloth. "Zander, honestly, I just wanted more time to think. You want me to act normal, right? Well, this is my normal way of getting out of class so I can chill out and clear my head. It doesn't help when you come busting in. You distract me and I don't need to be distracted right now."

He folded his arms against his slender, muscular chest, smiling smugly. "I distract you? How?"

I rolled my eyes. "Don't play dumb."

He seemed very amused at that one. "Pfft. Seems like someone becomes a little diva without her beauty sleep huh?" He smiled so widely his whole face lit up.

"You can thank yourself for that." The statement came out more curtly than I wanted it to.

His smile slowly faded as his eyes became more compassionate.

"I can imagine. The dreams must not be easy. The things you've probably seen would definitely paint another picture of me."

I sat there in silence. What could I say? He was right and he knew it, he didn't need me to confirm his suspicions. He took a couple steps closer, which I was *not* having. I got up to stand in front of the door.

"Look, my dad will be here soon, so you should go." I was proud that my voice sounded more confident than I felt.

"What you've been seeing, that's not who I am anymore. I just want to make sure you know that." He started towards me again.

"Can you just stand *still*?" I snapped. I didn't mean to, but him being so close to me was not a good idea. My defenses were weakening, which is exactly what I didn't want.

"I'm sorry." He looked down. "I'm drawn to you, I have this urge to be close to you. Sometimes I fear it will drive me mad." He slowly raised his eyes back up to meet mine. They had a longing in them that made me feel as though I'd become a standing pile of Jell-O. "I know you feel it too, Princess. That's what made you kiss me last night, isn't it?"

Oh boy, here we go! The moment I was dreading. I could only imagine the shade of red my face was. I crossed my arms, embarrassed.

"First of all, *you* kissed me."

"But *you* kissed me back." He countered.

"Second of all, stop calling me Princess! I'm just me, OK? Normal, ordinary, plain Jane, *me*!"

He eyed me with such a devious smile that my face went from red to deep crimson. "There's nothing ordinary about you, Princess."

"Ugh! Can you just *stop*?" I pinched the bridge of my nose in frustration. As long as I could avoid eye contact I could get a grip on myself.

"You are what you are, Angel, there's nothing you can do about it. Getting angry or pretending like it's not real isn't going to make it go away. I said act normal, not disown your history. You may not want to admit what you feel for me, but I know I'm right."

"So what if you are, Zander, we can't work! You can't even meet my *parents* for crying out loud!" The look on his face made waves of guilt wash over me. "Listen. What I saw last night shook me up. You weren't the same as you are now, that's true, but seeing you so vicious and empty is hard for me to get past. *I* may be able to overlook the things you've done in your past, but my parents? My *people*? You and I won't go over well at *all*."

He stared at me in silence for a moment. "What's done is done. But what is to come, neither you, nor I can predict." He took a step closer. He was the predator again and I was his prey. "I say we live in the moment."

My shield broke and I went to take a step closer to him, but he disappeared in a blur out the cracked door. The nurse came in a second later, smiling warmly at me.

"Your father's here, Angel."

She escorted me out to the car. My little spectacle must have been quite effective to get that kind of treatment. I had hoped she would allow me to walk myself which would've given me the chance to seek out Zander one last time, but that blew up in smoke. When I got in the car, Dad handed me a warm heated pillow to support my neck.

"Here, sweetie, it will help with the nausea."

I wanted to roll my eyes, but just played along. Once home, he made me a cup of tea, lit up a eucalyptus-scented incense and rubbed my temples with peppermint oil. I felt bad, him being the amazing dad that he is, trying to make his "sick" daughter feel better. But realistically I did feel like garbage emotionally, so this special treatment was in fact helping me to relax.

I felt my phone vibrate. It was a text from Julie.

What gives? Where did you die off to?

Sorry, I wasn't feeling well. I'm at home.

Well, lucky for you, I'm awesome! I got so much dirt on Zander today in class, you're going to freak!!

I bet I will, I thought. I should've known ditching would only give Julie the advantage she needed to be the queen snoop. Why would he even give in to her? He must've known that she would give me the full report afterwards. I smiled to myself, then instantly snapped out of it. I was doomed. What I felt for Zander was deeper than I thought. It has a mind of its own, one that rebels against everything I know on the outside to be wrong. I decided to keep it short with Julie so that she would give me space too.

K, tell me 2morrow, I'm going to try and rest up.

KK, feel better.

I buried my head under my pillow. This so-called "sick day" had to be used wisely. What I really needed to give me a boost was a peaceful sleep. I wondered how long the dreams would last. If they were really because of Zander, I wondered if I would eventually become immune to them based on how frequently we saw each other.

A crazy idea struck me: anytime I was sick, up all night coughing or sneezing, my parents would give me this tea that made me pass out. That's what I needed more than anything, to completely shut myself off from the world and just *sleep*.

"DAAAAAAAAD!"

Dad came in a moment later. "What is it sweetie? Do you need the garbage bin closer to your bed?"

"No. Can you make me some of that tea that you always give me whenever I can't sleep?"

"The lavender tea?"

"Yeah, I think that's the one."

"Sure."

He was back in ten minutes with the tea, filling up the room with its calming aroma. He sat down on the edge of the bed and handed it to me.

"Thanks, Dad."

His eyes were concerned. "You have been looking very tired lately. Have you not been sleeping, sweetie?"

If I didn't know the new information I did, I would have thought nothing of his question. But based on my newfound knowledge, I knew he was fishing to see if anything strange was happening to me. He must know that it's only a matter of time before I start acting weird because of this "breach." I hated lying to him, but I knew that I had to.

"I think there's something going around. I thought it was the tacos, but now that you mention it, I haven't been feeling too great these last couple days. I must be coming down with something." I added a little cough to emphasize my statement.

His brows wrinkled as he leaned forward to place the back of his hand on my forehead. "You feel fine to me, but if there is something going around, we should nip it in the bud before it gets worse. Drink up, love, get some rest." He softly kissed my forehead and started towards the door. He stood there for a moment indecisively before turning back to me. "Sweetie?"

"Yeah, Dad?" It came out breathy as I was blowing to cool down the tea.

"Is there anything you want to tell me?" His face was worried, but his eyes were serious.

My heart wrenched. There was so much I wanted to tell him, but I couldn't. I believed that Zander wanted to help me. As much as I tried to force myself not to trust him, something inside me told me I could. In fact, something else inside me didn't want to be separated from him either. He *knew* Sindrell. Without him we'd be running blind.

"Like what?"

"I don't know, anything?" He searched my eyes for comprehension.

"Not that I can think of." I tried to sound as passive as I could.

"OK. Well, you know I'm here if you ever want to talk about anything, even if it sounds strange or weird."

"I know, Dad." I forced a smile, feeling like he could see right through me.

He smiled back, but it didn't quite touch his eyes as he left my room. I sighed in relief, but it was short-lived. I knew nothing of what being an Oleah was all about or of the powers that we have. Mom and Dad were Oleah's the majority of their lives; they would be so much more in tune with their senses. I prayed that they couldn't pick up on my deception or feelings of guilt. They were humans now and most humans weren't too intuitive. My head was spinning again. The need to shut my mind off was greater than before. I blew harder on my tea, taking my first big gulp.

Once my cup was finished, within ten minutes I felt my eyes getting heavy. My head bobbed as I tried to watch the last bit of my show before sleep took me under.

* * * * *

I rolled over, briefly opening my eyes to see that it was dark outside. I felt refreshed and rested. It almost seemed foreign to me. I glanced at the clock. 4:30am. Whoa! I've been asleep for fourteen hours with no awful interruptions. I couldn't help but smile that my idea worked.

My stomach growled angrily in hunger. I definitely needed a snack. I went downstairs to search the fridge and found a plate wrapped in aluminum foil. Peeling the foil back, I peeked inside, and my mouth watered at the sight of chicken parmigiana. After I scraped up every last bit off the plate and downed a tall glass of milk, my sweet tooth craved something to indulge in after such a delicious meal. I decided on a large brownie square and headed back up to my room, satisfaction tickling me to my core. I sprawled out on the bed, stretching out all my muscles, cuddled up under the blankets and started flipping through channels.

There was never anything good on in the wee hours of the morning, just infomercials. I found myself drifting off again.

* * * * *

My dream was muddled with blurring colours. There were the sounds of shouts followed by a loud clanking of some type of blunt weaponry and ferocious growls. Over the background noise, there was a whisper that was just loud enough for me to decipher.

"Angel, you're OK, baby, shhhhhh." I couldn't tell if the voice was male or female, but it soothed me with its comforting mantra.

* * * * *

My eyes fluttered open, but to my surprise I was relatively calm. I sat up rubbing the sleep out of my eyes. These dreams, as awful as some of them may be, were a gift. I had to embrace them and the history that came with it. I didn't know if I would ever see Uforika again, but these dreams took me there, showing me the beauty and enchantment of the planet that was once my home.

Once I was ready for the day, I still had an hour to spare. I sat out on the back porch, sprawling out on one of the lawn chairs, taking in the early morning sunshine. The air was crisp and fresh. I inhaled deeply, soaking it all in. Before everything Zander told me, I would never have thought to appreciate the little things like these moments where I could slip away unnoticed and bask in the serenity of my surroundings.

"You look much better, Princess."

The sound of Zander's voice startled me and I sat upright, opening my eyes, searching the backyard. My heart was racing. He was too close, his presence would not go unnoticed.

"Are you crazy?" I hissed in a loud whisper to the open air.

He chuckled lightly and I stood up in aggravation, continuing to scan the area. He was putting himself at risk. Surely he of all people should know the consequences!

"Are you trying to get caught? Get out of here!" I practically barked the words out, making my way back inside. If my parents weren't just waking up, I would have slammed the door to emphasize my point.

"Looks like someone is feeling better." Mom stood on the other side of the island in the kitchen, taking a sip of her coffee.

"Hey, Mom," I tried not to sound as startled as I felt. "Yeah, I feel much better, that tea really helped."

I walked over to sit on a barstool. Mom pushed over the cereal box and a bowl towards me.

"I figured that much, you were completely comatose last night," she replied as she took the milk out of the fridge, handing it to me. "Did you and Zander make out?"

Panic shook me. Did she just say what I think she said? "What?"

"With the project." She seemed confused. "Did you not finish it? Isn't it due today?"

My whole body loosened. *DUH!* She knows I have a project due today, not that I've been making out with her nemesis. "Yeah, we finished everything. I'm banking on a really good mark on it."

Mom's face lightened. She loved academic talks, especially when it involved raising my average.

"That's great, honey! So, is he still bothering you or are you two OK now? Because you know if he's coming on too strong, you tell him he'll have to answer to your mother." I would've laughed, but she wasn't joking, so I settled on rolling my eyes instead.

"No Mom, he's cool. It's fine, Julie just over exaggerates."

Oh Mom, if only you knew, I thought. You'd lock me up for life and condemn me to an all-girls galaxy for the rest of my existence.

"I see. So will he be coming to the party?"

HA! "No."

There was no way in *hell* Zander could ever come here. He would stand out like a sore thumb. I imagined how it would go down: Zander walking in, Mom catching first sight of him, grabbing the knife from the kitchen drawer and charging at him full throttle. Happy birthday to me.

"Why not? Didn't you tell him about it?" She raised her eyebrows suspiciously.

"Yeah, he's going somewhere that day, so he can't come."

Her eyebrows drew together in a frown. "That's too bad. I would've liked to meet him and see what all the fuss is about."

No, no you wouldn't.

"I remember when I first met your father, I thought he was the most spectacular man I'd ever seen. He literally took my breath away." She blushed at the memory and I couldn't help but smile back. "I was so nervous when he started talking to me, I couldn't even put a proper sentence together. He was from an opposing tribe. My parents had originally arranged a marriage for me, but your father came along and messed it all up." She was practically giggling.

"Hold up. You were supposed to get married to some random guy?"

Mom rolled her eyes. "Can you believe it? I was so upset! He was such a boring guy, not even his looks could save him."

We both laughed at the poor fella's expense. I wondered in the back of my mind if she was telling the truth, but judging by the blushing, I'd say her recollections were pretty authentic.

"My parents were so upset with me. They said that your father was not up to standard. Can you believe it? They actually forbade me from seeing him."

"Are you *serious*?" I practically fell off my chair in shock.

"Yup, so you can imagine how they took it when I told them I didn't want to marry this other guy because I was in love with your father."

"What'd they do?"

"Well, they called off the wedding and at first my mother was extremely upset with me and wouldn't give her blessing for your father and I to marry, but eventually my dad made her come around." She smiled to herself, reminiscing. "Your father was a great leader in the tribe. He made my parents proud and ashamed that they ever doubted him."

Dad walked into the kitchen and it was obvious that he'd been eavesdropping. He came over, gently kissing Mom on the cheek. "I am pretty awesome. What can I say?"

Mom and I both broke out into laughter. She playfully hit him in his side and he raised his arms like a boxer would to block, then lunged for her. He locked her in an embrace, planting soft kisses on her cheek.

"I guess you are kind of awesome," Mom laughed breathlessly, leaning her head back into Dad's shoulder in defeat. He looked over to me with his full smile. It finally touched his eyes today.

"I see the tea did its job, huh, love?"

"Yeah, it sure did. Thanks, Dad. You're a great nurse while the doctor is still at work."

The mood was so perfect. This is the family I'm used to. We always got along so well. The past couple days had thrown me off more than I knew it ever could. Without them as my solid foundation I couldn't seem to grasp my equilibrium. We were a unit. I felt warmed by the merriment that was flowing in our house this morning and for the first time in three days, it genuinely felt like today would be a good day.

Dad grabbed a seat next to me on the other barstool, pouring milk into his cereal. Mom put her cup in the sink, looking over to me with a look that said she was up to no good.

"Eli, did Angel tell you that her partner for her geography project has the hot's for her?"

My eyes bulged out. *"Mom!"*

Dad stopped chewing and looked over at me with a blank expression. "Hot's huh?"

"O-M-G, you guys!"

Mom kept going. "According to Julie, he was being very forward with her, but Angel made it very clear to him that she was not interested." Mom continued provoking me with her canny smile.

Dad started chewing again, smiling back at me with a wink. "That's my girl."

"I was hoping we could get a look at this kid, you know, size him up at her party, but he's apparently not coming."

They were completely having a conversation between themselves, without a care in the world that I was sitting right there.

"I cannot believe you guys are talking about Zander right *now*!" I tried to laugh off my embarrassment.

"So this kid does have a name, huh?" Dad was totally playing Mom's game.

I was not about to talk about Zander with my parents. I tried to change the subject.

"Mom, are you going to make my favourite red velvet cake for the party?"

The look in her eyes told me she wasn't finished with me yet. "So, why aren't you interested sweetie? Is he not your type?"

I got up, ignoring them and put my bowl in the sink. I felt the flush in my cheeks. *He's totally my type.*

"Are you blushing?" Mom sounded more shocked than anything else.

"NO!"

"Oh my goodness, Eli, I think she actually likes him."

The teasing in her voice was gone. She was on to me. Damn that intuition! She didn't sound upset, just astonished. Dad looked over at me, mouth open. He had caught on too.

"I don't know *what* you guys are talking about. I do *not* like him."

Hearing myself say it, I knew the lie was weak. *Busted.* I turned on my heels, getting out of the kitchen as fast as I could, heading back up to my room to grab my backpack. *This was not part of the plan*, I chided myself. Hopefully they would just brush it off and leave me be. The less they knew about Zander the better.

On the way to school, Mom had the radio on the majority of the time. As we turned onto the street of the school, she turned down the music, swiveling around to give me an apologetic smile.

"You know, sweetie, your father and I were just teasing you this morning."

I continued to stare out the window, purposely avoiding eye contact. "Yeah, I know."

"It's OK if you have a crush, Angel." She encouraged.

Ugh! "Mom! I do *not* have a crush on him." My tone was stern, emphasizing every word.

She put up her hands defensively. "OK, OK, whatever you say."

Once we rolled up to school I was relieved to get out of the car and away from my mom's probing eyes. Julie was waiting by the curb, pouncing on me as soon as I got out.

"Bye, Mrs. Seriki!" She waved, waiting until my mom turned the corner to let it all out. "OK, so yesterday in class I was all like: 'What's taking Angel so long?' And Zander was all like: 'Maybe she's not feeling well, I hope she's OK', all concerned and *cute!*" I felt the tug of a smile trying to pull at my lips but fought it back. "Anyways, I told him about the party and he said that you told him about it already and that he's definitely coming –"

"Yeah, about that ... he's not."

"Not what?"

"Coming."

"Since when?" Her attitude shifted with a raised eyebrow to prove it.

"Yesterday, he can't make it anymore."

She crossed her arms. "Well, you have it wrong because he is totally coming, he said he was down to dress up in theme and everything!"

"Jewls." I said sharply.

"What?"

"He was just trying to be nice."

She gazed at me with annoyance. Something caught her eye over my shoulder, bringing forth a sparkle. I knew that look all too well as she glanced back at me. She was on a mission. She grabbed my hand, tugging me towards the football field. "We'll see about that."

I tried to pull away, but there was no stopping her. She resisted against me, only stiffening her hold on my hand, practically dragging me along with her.

"ZANDER! HEY!" She called out.

The fascinated grin on his face, made me want to run and lock myself in my locker. Mortified, I started tugging harder on Julie's hand in the opposite direction, hissing out to her.

"Jewls! What the hell?"

She continued to tune me out, dragging us closer to Zander. He was clearly enjoying every second of my humiliation.

"Hey!" Julie bounced, overjoyed.

"Hey. What are you ladies up to?" His entertained eyes met mine.

"Well, I was just telling Angel that you'll be one of the guests at her party, and she seems be under the impression that you're not coming. Care to clarify?"

He chuckled. "Yeah, I'll be there."

I stared at him, stunned.

"Thank you very much!" Julie said and she tugged on my arm, pulling me back in the other direction.

I looked back at him in indignation, mouthing the words: *What are you doing?* He waved goodbye smugly.

When we got inside the school, I yanked my hand away from Julie.

"What the hell was *that*, Jewls?"

"My point being proved. Anyways, back to my story –"

"Are you kidding me right now? You totally just embarrassed me in front of freaking *Zander*!" Aggravation set in.

She swept her hands in the air dismissing me. "Oh, come on Angel. Don't be such a drama queen."

I laughed out loud, livid. "DRAMA QUEEN? I would *never* have done that to you!"

"Will you relax? It's not like he said no."

"That's not the point! You just don't get it." I stormed off to our lockers. *So much for my good day.*

I felt the anger spreading, resonating deep within me. He *knows* he can't come to the party! What is he trying to pull, making me look stupid like that in front of Julie, and her having the audacity to call me out in front of him. I furiously threw my backpack down in my locker, catching my reflection in the inside mirror hanging on the door. A yellow tint began to spread in my eyes. I shut them firmly. I was too upset, I had to control myself or I'd be giving the whole school a show.

I drew in three long deep breaths, slowly opening my eyes to peek out again at my reflection. All traces of yellow were gone.

Julie finally caught up, looking like she finally realized why I was upset. "Don't get so angry, Angel. I'm sorry, OK?"

I grumbled. "Jewls, can you refrain from doing that again, please? I know you want to be Cupid and everything, but you don't have to embarrass me while you're at it."

Guilt plagued her features. "I know, it won't happen again."

I slightly smiled at her to ease the tension and went back to sorting through my books for the day.

She cleared her throat. "So, uh, can I tell you the rest of my story?" She smiled, embarrassed as I glanced over at her.

"Sure, go ahead."

She bounced giddily, clapping her hands. "OK! So at lunch I saw him hanging out by himself, and obviously since you weren't here, I was alone too, so I asked if I could join him." She instantly put up her hands. "Don't worry, he's all yours! I just wanted to find out some juicy details like if he had a girlfriend or was interested in anyone at school."

"Ugh, Jewls!"

"It was innocent, I swear. Anyways, he starts acting all shy, so of course that got me interested and I started probing him. It didn't exactly work, but get this! We started talking about the party again and I was telling him about our costumes and how I'm so excited to see you all dressed up because I think you're so pretty –"

"Oh my God." I cupped my face in my hands. "I'm going back home, I swear! I thought this was supposed to be *good*!"

"It is and it's *true*, so shut up! He's like: 'Yeah, she's quite stunning'."

I tried to hide the bashful smile that began forming on my lips, but couldn't help it. "He said that?"

"I *know*, right? But here's the best part!" Her shrieks were drawing attention to us, but Julie never cared what anyone thought of her. She was never insecure about herself, which is what I admired the most about her. "When he saw me looking at him, basically catching him in his confession, he got all shy so I blurted out, 'Why don't you ask her out?'"

"JEWLS!" I was mortified.

She smiled unapologetically, "Kill me later, OK, cause his response was, and I quote: 'I'm working on it!'" Her giddy jumping started again.

I knew all the circumstances as to why Zander and I couldn't work, all the reasons why we couldn't be together and yet, I still found myself smiling from ear to ear at the thought of us being a couple. Maybe in another life - where we are two normal teenagers - but not in this one. I couldn't help the pull I felt towards him. He was right, but that still doesn't make it right. Right?

We gathered all our things and headed off to class. I listened as Julie continued to make her attempts at convincing me to allow Zander to take me out. As we got to the end of the second hallway, my Zander alert went off. Great. There he was, leaning up against the geography class door.

Julie nudged me with her elbow, whispering under her breath, "Oh, he's waiting for you!"

I grumbled, knowing that Zander could hear every word. She smiled innocently at him as we parted ways. He took me in with his stare, a slow grin pulling at his lips.

"So nice to see you again, Princess."

This whole princess thing was really starting to get under my skin. "Can you stop calling me that?"

"Why?"

"Because I said so."

He raised his eyebrows, pretending to be shocked. "I can see that even with your beauty rest you're still a live wire."

I narrowed my eyes at him, crossing my arms. "What were you *thinking* this morning showing up at my house like that? Are you trying to make my parents go psycho?"

He looked thoroughly amused. "I wasn't at your house this morning, Princess."

"Really? That's the best you could come up with? Really, Zander?" My tone was heavy with sarcasm.

"I wasn't. I was down the street, honest."

"Then how could I hear you like that?" My rebuttal was fast.

"Telepathic conversations are just another perk of being superior." He breathed on his nails, buffering them on his chest. His responding smile punched me in the gut with its perfection.

I cleared my throat. "You have the project, right?" *Obviously, he has the project.* That one would go down in the books as one of my stupidest questions.

He nodded. "Don't you worry, you'll get your high mark."

I smiled sarcastically at him, starting for the classroom. He blocked the entrance with his arm. "Seems like Julie is trying to be Little Miss Matchmaker."

My heart began thumping against my chest. I wondered if he could hear it. "Yeah, and it seems like you're giving her enough ammunition to run with."

He leaned in closer, his voice a low whisper. "What's wrong with that?"

"You know everything is wrong with that." I tried my best to control my breathing and steady my heart rate.

His soft eyes searched mine as if he was waiting for me to say something else. His eyes lowered very slowly to my neck. Red tints danced within them. "Your pulse is racing. Do I make you nervous, Princess?"

I was locked in place, unable to come up with anything intelligent enough to use as a snide remark. "You intimidate me."

"Intimidate?" His eyes found mine again. "Why do I intimidate you?"

"Because … I don't know how to turn off this pull I have towards you either and it scares me."

"Maybe it's supposed to be on?"

I closed my eyes, unable to concentrate. "What good would come out of that?"

"Live in the moment, remember? " His voice was low and soft.

"Moments pass. What happens after? Is this worth the risk of all the consequences that would surface if we were to go public?" I opened my eyes to meet his gaze again and watched painfully as his expression transformed into hurt.

"I guess that's for you to decide." He lowered his arm, the brightness fading from his eyes, returning them to a dull auburn. He turned around and headed into the classroom.

Watching him walk away from me like that made me feel like the wind got knocked out of me. I turned my back to the classroom and took in a couple of deep breaths to stabilize myself, then made my way inside.

I took my seat beside Zander and cleared my throat.

"Listen, Zander, I'm sorry, I just…" My mind raced to find the right words but couldn't. I sighed, frustrated and upset at myself. "I don't know. I don't know much of anything anymore." I slumped in my chair.

Zander stared at the front of the classroom, saying nothing. I found myself staring at him, almost beckoning him to look at me. I barely heard a word Mr. Getty spoke throughout the entire class. I just kept staring, wanting him to acknowledge me. This morning he had carried his message to me by his thoughts and I was now determined to do the same. I focused all my energy on him, speaking his name in my head, telling my Oleah self to carry the words to him. I felt a tingle begin against my skin, and watched as Zander began to stir in his seat.

Stop it. He spoke the words in my mind.

It's working! I thought.

I bit down on my smile, overjoyed that I could actually do it. I pushed further, sending a new message to him.

Does this send signals to Sindrell?

He glanced at me from the corner of his eye, then returned his gaze back to the front of the class, sighed and shook his head no.

I smiled, continuing our telepathic conversation. *Are you mad at me?*

Nothing.

Hellooo?

He grinned to himself smugly. What a cocky jerk. Realizing that I wasn't helping my situation, just adding to how large his head was getting by the minute, I stopped and slumped deeper into my seat, crossing my arms tightly against my chest in annoyance.

Once Mr. Getty finished his lesson, the class had about fifteen minutes left to review, which translated to 'Sit and do nothing'. I saw Zander turn to stare at me in my peripheral vision. I kept my gaze forward, and he turned away, mimicking me in his seat.

He spoke into my mind. You're growing stronger every day. I never would have thought you could've figured this out on your own. Very impressive.

I snorted sarcastically, grunting under my breath. "Pfft, yeah right."

He continued to speak in my mind. I'm supposed to be mad at you, remember? Not the other way around.

"Ugh, you aren't even justified to *not* talk to me because I'm wary of dating you. Who even does that? That's such an incredibly human teenage boy thing to do." I hissed back to him aloud, turning to face him.

He kept his gaze forward, slowly bringing his index finger up to his lips. *Speak to me how I'm speaking to you.*

"Why?" I asked again aloud, growing more and more irritated by the minute.

He briefly glanced at me, his expression very ambiguous as if he couldn't decide whether to be shocked or upset as he spoke the words into my mind more sternly. *Because, this conversation is private.*

I felt the heat spread into my cheeks. I suppose he was right, this wasn't the type of conversation that should be for all to hear. I focused all my energy again on trying to tap into my Oleah self and transfer my words to Zander's mind. Once the tingling started against my skin, I knew I was ready once more.

I said I was sorry, but quite frankly I shouldn't even be sorry because you're upset at something so juvenile.

Zander unfolded his arms and turned to fully face me, placing his hand over mine. His eyes were honest and his expression shamed.

You're right. I'm still adapting to certain things, like not getting what I want when I want it. Forgive me.

I tried to glare into those auburn eyes with all the anger I had, but ended up softening my expression and half-smiling back at him. How does he do it? One minute I can't stand him and not even half a second later, there I am again wound up in his gravitational pull. He really was a predator. Dangerous in the worst possible way to an innocent bystander like myself. This is why he intimidated me, this is why I should run and never look back, block him out and forget he ever existed. But I knew for a fact that the idea of never having him in my life again made me sick to my stomach.

I continued with our "superiors only" conversation.

Explain something to me. Why is it that when my eyes change colour, it sends a signal to Sindrell, but this doesn't?

When you're upset you emit a different type of energy versus when you're calm. That same energy when you're upset starts to trigger the transformation, which is strong enough to stand out as something unusual to her.

I see. And on another note, how do you expect to come to my party? You of all people know that can't happen.

He grinned. I've been working on something that I just might be able to pull off.

Like what?

One useful thing that came out of my interactions with Sindrell was that I learned a few magic tricks. I can conjure up an illusion so that when your parents see me, they will see the face of someone else.

I gasped. Could he really do that? *What about the warning signals? They'll know that you're not from this world.*

Yes, well, I may be able to resolve that as well. Since your parents are technically human now, they would be susceptible to my spell versus if they were in their true Oleah form. Their mind will tell them I'm just an ordinary guy and their bodies will respond. It's physics really, the power of the mind.

When the bell sounded, he stood and turned to face me, holding out his curved arm to me. I hesitated for a moment, but decided to give in and link my arm with his as we set out into the hallway.

Julie appeared around the corner and instantly her eyes bulged. She looked to him, then to me, smiling so wide I felt like my cheeks were burning.

"What is this all about, guys? Going public?" The excitement in her tone was contagious.

I bit down on my cheek, trying to hold back my smile and play it cool. Julie stood there practically bouncing in front of us, waiting for a response. It dawned on me in that moment that I was too.

He glanced over to me with his side grin. "Just living in the moment."

For once I tuned out Julie's shrieks. In this moment it was just me and him.

He spoke into my mind. *This will work, Angel. We will work. You'll see.* He gently nudged me with his elbow.

Julie began rambling on about how cute we were together. I continued to zone her out, and answered, *We'll see.*

Deep down I couldn't deny my feelings, or how right the thought felt of us being together. If what he said was true and this spell of his works, I won't have to worry about my parents ever finding out about him. Well, for now at least, until we figure something else out.

After school Julie was surprisingly quiet on the way home. We dropped her off and she looked at me as if secretly passing a message that we had to talk. Literally not even five minutes after Mom and I got home, Dad told me that Julie was on the phone and said that it was urgent.

"Hello?"

I don't even think I heard her take a single breath, all I heard was a massive jumble of words coming at me in rapid fire.

"O-M-G, Angel! Tell me freaking everything! How did it happen? Did you take his arm? Did he take yours? Oh my gosh, did you see the way he smiled at you? Angel –"

"Whoa! Jewls, slow down, you're killing me here. One question at a time!"

She took in a deep breath and started again. "OK. Sorry, it's just that this is your first boyfriend, Angel, it's *huge*!"

"He's *not* my boyfriend, Jewls."

"Well, it certainly looks like it!"

I waited for my parents to slip away into the other room so that my full range of gossip could start. Once safely in the clear, I let it all out.

"OK, *fine*, I admit it! I'm majorly freaking out! I've known him for like four days and I feel like I've known him forever! He's *sooooooo* hot! I think I die a little every time he looks at me."

Julie giggled almost hysterically. "I know! I know! He's gorgeous, I am *so* jealous, I can totally see when you guys are together that it's deep. I can't even explain it, you guys just exude this energy. So tell me *everything*!"

I gave her as many juicy tidbits as I could. I lost track of time as we continued to obsess about Zander when Mom came down in her robe looking flabbergasted.

"Are you seriously still on the phone? Have you even *eaten* yet?"

I rolled my eyes. "*Yes*, Mom, I did, and this is a very important conversation if you don't mind."

She crossed her arms, making the term *if looks could kill* pop into mind.

"Angel. You guys see each other every single day. You've been monopolizing the phone for the past three hours! It's time to say goodnight."

"Three hours! Are you serious? Jewls, we've been on here for three hours!"

We both started cracking up. Mom's expression grew darker.

"OK, Jewls, I gotta go, we'll talk more tomorrow."

I hung up the phone, and slid past Mom, avoiding her menacing grimace as I headed up to my room. I bumped into Dad at the top of the stairs, who greeted me with a smile that told me he knew I'd been talking about boys on the phone. I knew Dad would not be thrilled, but he would accept the fact that I'm at the dating age a lot better than Mom ever would, even if it was with just an ordinary guy. Zander could definitely handle the heat, but the thought alone of it coming out to my parents, sent shivers running through me.

Keeping this thing I have with Zander a secret was not going to be easy. In fact, this was going to be the hardest thing of my life, apart from the villain sorceress trying to kill me. After all, it's all just another day in the life of an ordinary girl.

Chapter 8: Party Time

I woke up in a cold sweat, fear clenching my stomach, sending waves of nausea crashing down on me. For once, I actually wished that what I was experiencing was due to another dream, but no. It was far worse. There was no waking up from this reality. Today was the day of my party. All the preparations over the last two weeks, the costume fitting, the RSVPs, the catering, and the DJ was all for me. I was to be the center of attention and that was a fear that shook me to my core. The last couple days leading up to today have been a blur. When I wasn't running with Mom to grab last-minute trinkets, I was here with Julie setting up the décor to ensure that the theme was precise down to the last detail. Never in a million years would I have ever thought that I would become so wrapped up in all this, but the truth is that this themed party was a way for me to allow Mom and Dad to feel like they're back home, and that was a gift I would do anything to give.

Tonight was huge for them, and for me. For them, I was crossing over into adulthood, and for me Zander would put his own preparations to the ultimate test. If all went according to plan, he would officially be introduced to my parents. Another shiver ran over me at the thought. I hoped and prayed that this would work. These last two weeks with him at school have been a fairy tale that I still can't believe is real. Being with him makes me feel powerful and confident, and dare I say *beautiful*. He teaches me every day about the Oleahs and the powers they possess, guiding me through the things I don't understand and helping me to tap into my Oleah self to get stronger each day without being noticed by Sindrell.

"Angel, sweetie, it's time to get up. We have to get started on your hair." Mom said, knocking on the door.

I rubbed the sleep out of my eyes and wiped the sweat off my face as I made my way to the shower. "I'm heading to the bathroom as we speak!"

"That's what I like to hear." Mom responded.

After my shower, I made my way downstairs in my robe with a towel wrapped around my head, comb in hand. Mom stood on the other side of the island in the kitchen with my usual breakfast waiting for me.

"Did you use the leave-in conditioner?"

"Mmmhmm," I garbled through a mouthful of cereal.

Mom stood looking at me with admiring eyes, smiling to herself. She came over to me and cupped my face, wiping away the excess milk from my mouth.

"You are so beautiful, my precious, sweet girl. Happy birthday." She leaned down to kiss me on both cheeks.

I rolled my eyes. "Thanks, Mom."

She started combing through my hair and parting it in sections so she could begin braiding the top half of my head. The bottom would stay out so the braids could fall and intertwine in my curls. I loved the way the braids looked when Mom did them. She was quite the hairstylist when she wanted to be.

She began braiding the first parted section. "So, I got a last-minute RSVP from Joan so that brings our total to a hundred and fifty."

I nearly choked on my cereal, spitting it back into the bowl.

"WHAT? A hundred and *fifty*? How is that even possible, Mom? I only handed out twenty invites!"

She carried on casually as if I hadn't just been choking. "Yes, you handed out twenty invites to your friends, and I handed some out to my close friends at work, and to some of your father's friends and close business associates, and well, we couldn't be rude and have a party without sending out an invite to the neighbours."

I instantly lost my appetite. "I'm gonna throw up."

Mom just brushed me off. "Oh, please, Angel, enough with the dramatics."

"This was *not* part of our agreement, Mom!" I whined. "I said I only wanted *ten people*. I compromised to twenty for Julie, and that was pushing it! It's bad enough that you guys made such a big deal about it, but now I have to deal with a hundred and fifty eyes looking at me? Just kill me now!" I threw my hands up to emphasize my point. Maybe I was being a little dramatic, but I couldn't help it. Mom totally played me.

"Sweetie, seventeen is a big deal, OK? Maybe not to you, but if we were back in our village, tribes from all over would've come to celebrate your passage into adulthood. You would've been blessed by the elders and showered in gifts. They would've slaved away for months beforehand just to make you the perfect stage that you would sit on so that everyone could come up to you and wish you well." There was the slightest crack in her voice.

My heart wrenched as I turned to face her. She gave me a slight smile, staring back with glossy eyes. "It would've been beautiful."

The weight of her sacrifice swept over me. With my voice barely audible, I started, "Mom, I -"

She cut me off, laughing to herself and wiping her eyes. "Look at me getting all blubbery. I'm sorry, sweetie. I should have told you. It's just today is truly something to celebrate. There was once I time I wasn't sure if your father and I would get to see you turn seventeen –"

"Mom –"

"No, no, let me finish." She cupped my face again, looking me dead in the eyes. "We've been blessed, Angel. More than you'll ever know. To be here together, and to be safe; others were not so lucky. I'm sorry that I'm getting all mushy, but I'm just so grateful to see my baby become a woman." She leaned in to kiss my forehead.

As she leaned back to smile at me, tints of yellow began swirling in her eyes. The sight almost threw me off guard, but I kept my composure together. She clearly had no clue that she was giving me an eye show. I had to lighten the mood, to get her mind off of it. If she caught a glimpse of herself in the mirror, she would know that I saw and had not reacted, which would not be good.

I hugged her tightly, thanking her for everything and got her talking about the costumes she made for Julie and I. Anytime we talked about it she would light up and go on and on about how amazing the quality and texture of the fabric was, how she almost thought they wouldn't be ready on time and so on.

As she got into it, I began to worry about Zander's plan. Occasionally glancing back at her to check her eyes and thankfully, after a couple of minutes all traces of yellow were gone. I let out a little breath in relief, closing my eyes to listen as she continued on about how amazing the costumes looked while working away at my hair.

When she finally finished my hair, I couldn't help but gawk at myself in the mirror. The braids that contoured my face were intertwined with little shells and pearls, my hair in the back hung in perfect tendrils, sparkling in the light from the glitter hairspray Mom put in. I felt pretty. I had about an hour until Julie came by to do my makeup. I decided now would be the best time to talk to Zander and tell him what happened with my mom. I called his phone, which had become our secret signal to each other when we needed to talk.

You rang? His voice sounded in my mind.

I couldn't help the smile that accompanied hearing his voice. We'd been practicing telepathic conversations with each other throughout the last couple weeks so that we could have our secret convos when I was at home without having to worry that my parents would be eavesdropping. I closed my eyes and focused my energy.

Not even a minute later. I like that.

Well, it is an important day, so I figured I should make myself available for the woman of the hour. I could hear the smile in his voice. *Getting nervous for the party?*

Nervous? No, more like sick to my stomach. My mom has a hundred and fifty people coming!

Well, aren't you the popular one? he teased.

I emphasized my unimpressed tone. *Looks like it.*

You'll be fine, don't worry. I'll be there to make fun of you.

I chuckled to myself. *How sweet. Have you been working on the spell?*

Every day. His tone was very self-congratulatory. Should go off without a hitch.

I felt the butterflies start to flutter in my stomach. *I hope so, but we may have a problem.*

Oh?

Yeah, my mom got really emotional earlier and her eyes started to turn yellow. Is that bad?

Hmmm. His tone was more serious. It definitely complicates things. The reaction that your mom had to me a couple weeks ago must have triggered her powers. She may have started having the dreams.

I stiffened. *That's bad. That's very, very bad.*

There's no way to tell, but if that is the case, she knows how to use her powers to her advantage. She's going to be on guard and may detect me before I even set foot in the house. How does she seem? Restless? Extra secretive?

I ran through her behaviour this last week in my mind and she'd seemed genuinely happy. *No, she's been great. Really excited, super happy. I haven't seen her frown once all week.*

That could be a good sign. Seeing me then may have just triggered her powers, but not set them off because it was only the one time. There's no way of knowing, though.

The butterflies in my stomach got more intense. *What do we do?*

Nothing.

So, you're still coming tonight? What if she's been having the dreams? It'll be a disaster! Surely he wasn't that reckless.

Don't worry, I have a back-up plan. Can't wait to see you later.

I felt the telepathic connection beginning to slip away. *Wait! Zander! Zander?*

Silence.

What's your back-up plan?

I crossed my arms, irritated that he could just shut me out. In order for our minds to connect to one another we must be open to receiving. I, of course, was always open but Zander puts up a block most of the time to prevent Sindrell from getting into his thoughts. I understood his apprehension, but it's still annoying that he can just cut me off. I was still fuming when Mom came in the room.

"What's wrong, sweetie? Why do you look so frazzled?"

"It's nothing," I sighed. "Just can't find something, that's all." I did the best I could to fix the look on my face.

"What were you looking for? Maybe I can help?"

"No, it's nothing, don't worry, Mom. I probably left it at school anyways." I glanced at the costumes draped over her forearm. "So, let's see them!"

A wide smile spread across Mom's face, lighting up her eyes as she laid the costumes down on my bed. Originally the costumes were supposed to be two pieces but she merged it into one. It was stunning. The soft suede skirt was a deep honey brown with tan stitching. Attached to the front and back were what looked like thick black leather pieces that connected the top to the skirt, leaving the sides open. The leather-like material had a tiny sparkle to it in the light and would tie up around my neck to be a V-shaped halter. There were also thick black strips that had honey-brown suede paw prints around them and dangling strips of feathers and tiny shells that would go around our arms above our elbows. It was truly a work of art.

I smiled widely. "Mom, these look amazing!" I leaned in to touch the fabric of the skirt and at first contact with my hand, an image of an Oleah woman wearing an exact replica came into my mind. I gasped, taken aback by the vision. It became clear then that Mom had duplicated our tribe's clothing down to a "tee". I looked at Mom, completely blown away.

"What is it? Everything OK, sweetie?" She eyed me cautiously.

I gathered myself quickly. "Yeah, they're gorgeous! But they look really expensive, Mom. How much did you spend?"

She fanned the air with her hand. "Oh, please! You'd be surprised at the type of fabric you can find for next to nothing when you know where to look. In fact, when you take into account that I made them myself, I actually ended up saving money versus if I would've given them to a seamstress."

I hugged her tightly and I heard the door open downstairs. Julie's voice echoed through the house.

"The party's here!"

I should have known Julie would show up early. She hasn't knocked on our door since I met her. She's always just walked right in, knowing that she was like family to us.

"We're up here Julie! " Mom called back. She looked at me, worried, lowering her voice to whisper. "I should run and go get my earplugs and armour. She's going to lose her mind."

I giggled as Julie came into my room, her eyes instantly widening.

"OH. MY. GOSH. ANGEL! *YOUR HAIR!*" Her voice rose about three octaves. "It looks incredible!" She looked at Mom. "I want braids too!"

Mom choked back a laugh. "I can give you two french braids if you like."

Julie started her usual bouncing and clapping followed by little squeals in between. "Deal! Can you add in the shells and feathers? We have to be consistent!"

I bit back my smile, looking at Mom who just smiled back at Julie, waiting for her to completely erupt. Julie came in closer to touch my braids, catching a glimpse of the costumes on the bed. She did a double take, completely awestruck.

"HOLY SHIT!" she screamed, instantly covering her mouth with both hands.

I burst into laughter at the look of complete shock on her face at how loud she had just cursed in our house. Mom looked a little stunned, but began laughing hysterically with me while Julie began what could only be described as hyperventilating.

Mom approached Julie, resting her hand on her shoulder. "Breathe sweetie, I can't have you fainting on me."

"Water. I need water." Julie managed to choke out between gasps.

I quickly ran downstairs, chuckling to myself to fill up a cup of water and rushed back upstairs, handing it over to Julie, who was now sitting down on my bed with her head in between her knees. She quickly chugged the whole glass, finally catching her breath.

"Better?" Mom asked, taking the cup away from her.

Julie nodded her head and looked back at the costumes lying undisturbed beside her. "I'm so sorry, for a second there I thought I was going to die from beauty overload! Mrs. Seriki, these are incredible!" She stood up, locking me in a bear hug. "Angel, we are going to look like superstars!"

Her voice rose higher in octaves again as she began laughing hysterically, still not letting me out of her vice grip.

"Jewls, you're stifling me."

She let me go, holding on to my shoulders, still giggling to herself. "Oops. Sorry."

Mom just stared at Julie in awe. "My goodness, child, you are crazy. Come, let's get your hair started before you break something."

Mom took extra long on Julie's hair so that she could fully calm down before having another "episode". It seemed to work. She just kept stroking the fabric of her costume as if it was her own personal prized pet. Once her hair was finally done, equipped with the same shells and feathers I had in mine, Julie opened up her makeup bag and got right down to business. Of course I wasn't allowed to see until she was finished, having to sit there and watch as Julie paused each time to take a better look and my mom stood beside her, tilting her head in the same direction. Had I not been so anxious to see, I would have thought it was hilarious.

"OK, that should do it." Julie leaned in one last time to add the final touches to my lips, standing back with Mom to give me their last appraisal.

Mom uncrossed her arms. "Julie, I must hand it to you. You have a natural talent. She looks absolutely beautiful." Her voice broke near the end.

"I know, right? Totally nailed it! Angel, you look amazing."

I stood up to stretch out my neck and arms, eager to see myself in the mirror. Julie side-stepped, blocking my view.

"Oh no you don't, you're not finished yet."

"You just said I was done."

Julie looked disbelievingly at Mom. "Is she for real?"

Mom nodded her head back at Julie. "Mmm hmm."

"Am I missing something here? My hair's done, makeup's done….Why can't I see myself?"

"Ugh! Obviously because you need to see the final picture in your costume, silly." Julie crossed her arms looking at me as if anyone would have figured that out.

"Are you serious? C'mon! Let me see, the party isn't for another hour and a half. You seriously don't expect me to put on the costume *now*, do you?"

My statement was met with blank stares from both Mom and Julie. I started to laugh nervously, but their expressions remained the same.

"Ugh, fine." I stretched my arm out for Julie to hand me my costume.

Instantly their faces lit up with excitement.

"So where am I supposed to change since I can't look at myself?"

They stared at each other for a moment. Mom began to signal to Julie with her head movements, nudging in one direction. As Juie's eyes met the space in consideration, my eyes followed to my closet.

"You've got to be kidding me." I laughed.

Mom smiled back, scrunching her nose as if she was looking at a baby whose cheeks she wanted to squeeze. "There's nothing wrong with the closet, sweetie. Now go on, get in there."

"Why can't I just change in the bathroom? You guys can cover the mirror, I won't peek!" I whined.

Julie approached me, casually pushing me into the closet, "Listen, Angel, we love you and everything, but at this point, you can't be trusted."

"What!" My bug-eyed expression went from Julie to Mom. "Mom!"

Mom smiled, giving me a little wave as Julie positioned me in the closet, shut the door and turned on the light. "Hurry up, honey, we're waiting."

Luckily I had a small walk in closet. I held up the costume with both hands and eyed it with awe. My heart rate began to speed up. I was just as excited to see myself.

I stepped into the skirt, pulling up the halter to tie at the back of my neck. The fabric felt like silk gliding over my skin. I gazed down at myself, trying to see how it looked as I put on the arm bands. I straightened out the fabric of my skirt and took in a deep breath.

"I'm ready."

Mom opened the door and stood there, stunned. Julie stood closely behind with her mouth open. I felt my heartbeat pounding loudly in my head, deafening me in the silence that filled the room.

"Well ..." I looked at them, starting to get agitated.

"Eli! Get in here!" Mom screamed out, never breaking her gaze from me, eyes teary.

I started to move towards the mirror but Julie lightly pushed me back, breaking her deer-in-headlights gaze. "Just wait."

Dad came in the room, looked over to me and stood beside Mom, awestruck. "Oh, Angel." His eyes glossed over as Mom linked arms with him smiling widely.

I couldn't take it anymore. I walked over to the mirror to meet the reflection that I almost didn't recognize. My makeup was flawless with a deep, chocolate brown smoky eye shadow that made my eyes pop, shimmery bronzer with hints of blush to give me a natural glow and neutral lips. The costume accentuated my curves perfectly, the skirt rested right on my hips and the halter hung loose enough on my chest for me to still feel comfortable. The neutral colours gave my skin a rich tone that really played up the feathers and shells in my dark hair. I felt a smile tug at my lips. I'd never seen myself look this done up before and I actually felt beautiful. I reminded myself of my mother. I felt confident and strong in the costume, looking like an Amazonian princess.

Julie flung herself on to me, hugging me tightly from behind "Angel, you're smoking hot! I cannot wait to see the look on Zan-"

"How about we get you into your costume too, Jewls?" I cut her off, turning around to face her. My expression told her that we don't speak about boys in front of my parents. She caught on quickly, smiling and grabbing her costume.

"Good idea, I'll be right back!"

As Julie closed the bathroom door Mom approached me. "My little Angel, you're absolutely perfect."

"Thanks, Mom." I felt my smile widen, the excitement was starting to set in.

Dad came up and hugged me tightly. "Seeing you in that outfit touches my heart in ways I can't describe Angel."

I hugged him back tighter, feeling a lump begin to form in my throat, knowing exactly how he must feel. "I'm so proud to wear this, you guys. I really am."

"OK, where are the tissues?" Mom laughed, grabbing the tissue box off the counter and dabbing her eyes. "Oh, I almost forgot, I have one more thing for you."

I looked over to Dad, trying to get him to tell me what it was, but he shrugged his shoulders in confusion. A moment later Mom came back in the room with a necklace that looked handmade. It had a thick brown string and what looked like claws and feathers hanging from it. Dad took in a short breath at the sight of it, looking at Mom, who smiled widely back at him.

"This is a gift for you from one of our dearest friends back in the village. When you were a baby, we always had to practically tear you off of him. He loved you very much, and would have wanted you to wear this today."

As she slid the necklace over my head, a blurry vision of what looked like an Oleah soldier flashed into my head, his hands placing the necklace into my mother's hands. I looked down at the necklace, grasping the claws tightly.

"They're lion claws. All the soldiers from our tribe wore them as a tribute to all the fallen soldiers. The feathers represent purity and the string represents strength."

I hugged Mom tightly, my voice soft as I tried to hold back tears. "Thank you, Mom. For everything you've ever done for me."

Dad joined in to form our family group hug.

"Awwwww! You *guys*!" Julie's voice shrieked.

We all looked over at her as she struck a pose at the bathroom door, giving us her best duck face. "How do I look?"

"Oh my gosh, Jewls, you look amazing!"

She truly did. Her dark hair and blue eyes made her look like an Amazonian version of Wonder Woman.

"I know!" She squealed giddily as we both started jumping up and down.

"Yeah, that's our cue to get out of here," Dad laughed, covering his ears.

"Right behind you, honey!"

As soon as they left the room, Julie grasped my shoulders, leaning in to me with her voice low.

"Zander is going to lose his mind! He won't be able to keep his hands off you!"

I turned back to face the mirror, taking it all in with a deep breath. "You think so?"

"I *know* so!"

Giving myself one last look over, I mentally hoped that Zander's appearance tonight went off without a hitch.

"C'mon, Jewls. Let's get this party started."

* * * * *

Two and a half hours in, the party in full swing, it seemed like every one was having an amazing time. The compliments didn't stop on how good I looked, or how crazy amazing the décor was. The backyard was buzzing with chatter, laughter and awe as the drummers filled the air with their vibrations that had everyone dancing along. My parents would occasionally pull me over to introduce me to work colleagues who would rave about my beauty. To say my parents were in their glory was an understatement. I hadn't seen them this happy or carefree in what seemed like forever. The energy in the atmosphere had me feeling jovial myself, dancing alongside Jewls as the DJ started up.

I caught Jewls scanning the crowd. She looked over at me with a huge smile, shouting over the music. "This is so going down as the best party ever!"

I scanned the crowd too, absorbing everything, "I know! I wish Hector could've been here, he would've loved this!"

Julie pouted. "I know. Too bad he couldn't make it. We should make plans with our parents to get out to British Columbia soon for a visit."

"We totally should!" I continued to scan the crowd, very aware that everyone that was supposed to be here was, except for the one person I wanted to see the most. I felt a sting of worry as I wondered if he was going to show up at all. I understood that there was a slight chance he may not come if the spell didn't work and tried not to be disappointed, but I couldn't help it. I wanted him to be here.

Jewls must've caught the change in my expression. "Hey! He'll be here, don't worry."

I smiled back at her and continued to dance. After about twenty minutes on the dance floor, Jewls and I went to the punch bowl to rehydrate.

"HOLY CRAP! Parents! Meeting! Zander! Holy crap!" Jewls shouted, grabbing my arm.

It felt like my heart was doing acrobats in my chest as I followed her gaze to see Zander standing face to face with my parents. Panic set in, and before my mind could register what was happening, I was beside him.

Mom reached out to shake his hand, smiling widely. "Ahhh, the infamous Zander."

Relief swept over me. It worked. The spell worked.

Zander reached out to shake Dad's hand. "It's such a pleasure to meet you both. Thanks so much for having me."

"Glad we could finally meet you, young man. We've heard a lot about you." Dad's handshake was followed by a pat on the back and a wink to me.

"Oh my gosh, do not listen to them. I don't even know what they're talking about." I felt my cheeks growing redder by the second.

Zander chuckled. "All good things I hope."

Dad pulled Mom under his arm. "So, Zander, tell us about yourself."

I stood there in awe watching and listening to Zander woo my parents with stories of his academic background at Eastern Mills. He was clearly making sure the impression he was making was a good one.

Mom surprised me with how cool she was with all of this. She was beaming. "My, my, Zander, you're quite the catch aren't you? These days kids your age don't appreciate the arts and culture anymore. It's such a breath of fresh air to see a young man like yourself so well-educated and passionate about it."

"Thank you, Mrs. Seriki. I have been quite blessed to have the opportunities that have been given to me."

I couldn't help but wonder what my parents' perception of Zander was with his spell in full effect. Did he have dark hair to them? Or was he blonde? Did he keep his auburn eyes or did he give himself a different shade? Was he tall? It thoroughly intrigued me. I wished I could see through my parents' eyes just for a moment so I could perhaps see the way Zander saw himself.

"Angel?" Zander asked, looking at me expectantly.

"Huh?" I had zoned out.

He chuckled, looking at my parents. Mom reposed his question.

"Zander asked you if you would like to dance."

"Oh." I hadn't realized that the DJ had switched to slow ballads.
"*Oh!* Uh …" I looked at my parents cautiously. Mom gave a slight nod of her head followed by warm smile. "Uh, sure. Yeah."

Zander took my hand and excused us as he led me to the dance floor. I turned back to my parents again in complete awe that they were allowing me to dance with a boy! They stared back, smiling, then eventually returned to socializing with the guests. Julie was still standing frozen by the punch bowl, watching with her mouth hung wide open.

As Zander lightly pulled me in by the waist, entwining his free hand with mine, I looked up to him in shock.

"Holy crap, how strong is your spell? You have my parents in La La Land!"

He flashed me that wide smile I had come to adore. "Is it that hard to believe that I'm just a people person?"

"Uh, yeah right."

"The only spell your parents are under is just hiding my true face. Their feelings are genuine. Promise."

I glanced back over to them, watching as they chatted with some of the neighbours.

"This doesn't seem real." I gazed up at Zander, smiling widely. "How did they not sense you?"

"That's what took me so long. I couldn't remember how to block energy in the air. But as you can see, I figured it out." His smile was warm, but short-lived as his expression became more serious. "You look absolutely beautiful tonight, Princess."

I blushed, smiling back. "Still calling me Princess, huh? I thought we were over that."

"Nope. It's what you are. In fact, you should command that respect from me."

"Ha!" I laughed.

His eyes entranced me with their honesty. "Angel, I'm serious. I don't deserve to be here, yet still you accept me, knowing my past. Somehow I'm going to make all the wrongs of my past right with your family. I promise."

The charge between us made all the hairs on my arm stand upright. I had no idea what the future held for us, but with his spell working as well as it was tonight, the possibilities were endless. He was right. We *could* work. We *could* be together. I leaned my head onto his chest, soaking up the moment and he stiffened instantly. It felt as if every muscle in his body had become stone. I quickly looked up at him, concerned, watching as he winced as if he were in pain.

"Zander? Are you OK?"

He shut his eyes tightly, letting out a low, laboured grunt, pulling away from me casually to not draw attention to himself. He walked away through the crowd to the side of the house. I quickly looked around to see if anyone had noticed. Thankfully no one had except Julie. As I started walking towards the side of the house, she joined me.

"Everything OK?"

I had to come up with a lie quickly so she wouldn't follow. "Yeah, he realized he doesn't have his keys and thinks he dropped them when he was getting out of the car out front. I'm just going to help him look."

She looked at me skeptically. "You guys trying to be alone, huh?" A devious smile formed on her lips as she raised her eyebrows up and down.

I returned her smile. "Be on the lookout for me, OK?"

She raised her hand to salute me. "Aye, aye, captain. I want full details when you come back!"

I began walking backwards. "I promise."

As I got closer to the side of the house, I picked up the pace. I rounded the corner to find Zander leaning with his head against the brick, eyes closed, breathing heavily. His breaths sounded animalistic, as if he were a bear.

"Hey," I continued to approach him slowly, my mouth becoming dry as I felt adrenaline and fear pumping through me. "What's wrong?"

He put a hand up as a warning not to come any closer as he continued to focus on his breathing. I stood in place, watching his face morph in pain. Cold currents began to hit me, greater than any I'd yet experienced. Something was terribly wrong.

"Zander, talk to me. What's going on? Is it the spell?"

He growled in a deep feral tone. "We have to get out of here." He turned to me, grasping the wall for support, his eyes bright red. Shakily, he slowly moved towards me. Whatever was happening to him was draining him. Although I was consumed with fear, I rushed to him, wrapping his arm around my shoulder to support his weight.

"Tell me what to do!" My voice trembled with panic.

He steadied himself, closing his eyes. "Just give me a minute."

He took in three deep breaths and pulled away from me to stand on his own. When he reopened his eyes, they were back to normal. He seemed in control again. For only a moment, I saw fear in his eyes, but they quickly went cold.

"There's no time to explain, we need to get your parents and leave immediately."

Dread coursed through me. "Zander, what's wrong?"

He balled his hands into fists, clenching his jaw. "It's Sindrell. She's found us."

Chapter 9: Mine

I barely had the time to register what I'd just heard. Zander grabbed my hand, beginning to lead us back to the party.

"Whoa! Wait!" I pulled away from him. "What do you plan on telling them?"

"Listen very closely, Princess. If I don't give myself up to your parents now before they start to feel my presence and try and convince them that I'm on their side, Sindrell will hone in on our location and it will be too late. An all-out war will begin. Is that what you want? *War?* You have no idea what Sindrell is capable of or the power she has! Your parents will be doomed, and if we try to run, she'll use your parents to lure you back to her. There's no winning here if I don't get your parents up to speed and on board. Do you understand?"

The combination of the grave expression on his face with the severity of his tone sliced into me. I wrapped my arms around myself, hoping it would comfort me in some way. The weight of my reality was setting in. Like a steel ball latched to my ankle, there was no escaping it. I looked up at Zander and slowly nodded my head in agreement. He turned and started walking back to the party again. Before he could round the corner, he stopped abruptly, looking to the ground, then to me, eyes wide.

The ground began to shake violently beneath us. I listened as the sound of glasses breaking and screaming started from the party. The fence began collapsing and windows started to shatter on the homes around us as the earthquake continued to deface everything. I couldn't move. Fear had paralyzed me. It was as if everything was happening around me in slow motion. I watched the roofs cave in, followed by dust and debris filling the air. The hard cement beneath me began to crack open, splitting apart the walkway. I felt myself being knocked violently to the ground, watching in horror as part of the roof landed where I was just standing. The force of hitting the ground snapped me out of my daze. Zander was on top of me, eyes bright and wild.

"Angel, can you hear me? Are you OK?" He grasped my shoulders firmly.

I blinked away the tears, nodding, using his grip to steady me as the ground continued to shake. In that moment, Mom rounded the corner, frantic. When her eyes locked in on us, they began to glow yellow. Her stance became deadly, curling her lips back to expose razor sharp canine teeth. She rounded her back as if she were about to start a race, her hands curled inwards with thick pointed claws. An inhuman growl cut through air.

"Get away from her." She spoke the words slowly, laced with acid.

The hatred that contorted her face made her unrecognizable to me. She was out for blood and intended on ensuring its outcome. Zander rose, slowly lifting both hands up in submission. The quake finally ceased.

"I mean her no harm." As he stood, he very slowly and deliberately put one hand down to me.

I trembled, looking at Mom, who never once took her hateful glare off Zander. My heart was beating deafeningly fast. I couldn't seem to catch my breath.

Dad quickly came around the bend, eyes already lit. They were so in tune and in control of their powers. When his eyes met mine they were filled with fear and distress. My heart shattered. That look would haunt me for the rest of my life.

His arms were scratched and bloody, his hair and face full of dust. When his eyes left mine to meet Zander's, his face became stone and he spoke through clenched teeth.

"Red."

Zander still held out his hand to me. I slowly reached for it with shaky hands and Mom let out a roar that terrified me to my core. She took a step closer, but Dad held her back, speaking in her mind. *He has the advantage. We cannot attack until we have her out of harm's way.* I had to use this opportunity to show them that he was not the enemy.

He won't hurt me, I told them.

This line of communication was different with them, easy and effortless. Their bewildered eyes met mine. I nodded to them as I took Zander's hand for support and he lifted me up to stand beside him. Mom jerked forward with another growl and Dad restrained her again.

My stomach twisted with anxiety. I tried my best to ground myself so that I could come across confidently to my parents, but despite my efforts, my words came out shaky as I spoke them aloud.

"I – I know everything. Please, trust me, he wants to help us. Sindrell knows where we are and he's the only one with a direct link to her who can hide us."

Mom spat out so vehemently it made me flinch. "You have *no idea* who he *is*, Angel, or what he's done! He's manipulated your mind, he cannot be trusted!"

I locked my eyes on Dad, hoping I could get through to him. "He's had ample opportunity to bring me to Sindrell and he hasn't! He's chosen to help me. He taught me about my powers and how to use them. Why would he want to make me stronger if he wanted me dead? Dad, please, trust *me* if you don't trust him. We have to get out of here!"

Dad looked from me to Zander, his face still locked in a scowl as he continued to hold Mom back.

Zander spoke quickly and confidently. "Sindrell hasn't penetrated Earth's atmosphere yet. If she had, the queen would have already fully transformed by now. She knows that we're in Ontario, but not the exact location."

Mom countered hatefully. "How would she have figured all this out if you weren't helping her, traitor?"

Zander seemed to hesitate for a moment before speaking. "The spell I used tonight to conceal my face was very powerful. I thought it would be safe or I would never have tried it. I don't know how, but it acted as a beacon for her to locate me and tap into my mind again."

Mom growled, lunging forward again. "LIES! You knew what you were doing, you led her straight to us!" Dad continued to tighten his grip around her.

Zander continued. "That's not true! Listen to me. She uses available power as her source, the energy that you are exuding is feeding her as we speak and giving her exactly what she needs to cross into the atmosphere. If you stay here thinking that Coral will help, you will be doomed!"

Mom narrowed her eyes mistrustfully. "How convenient that you want us to shut off our powers. Do you take me for a fool, boy?"

"You don't believe me? That earthquake was her trying to get through. I *know* you felt her, just as I did! She won't give up. If she breaks through, she'll be able to find us in minutes. Her powers have grown tremendously! She plans to open a portal to all of Kindren and block all portals from Uforika. Not even Coral will be able to stop her. If we all act now and leave, it will throw her off balance and give us some more time to figure out a plan of action. Like it or not, I'm your best shot at survival."

My parents looked from Zander to each other. Dad loosened his grip on Mom, turning to gaze at me with defeated eyes before he returned his steely glare back on Zander.

"How do we get out of here?" He spoke between clenched teeth.

"I don't know the extent of the damage the earthquake has caused, but our best bet will be to get as far away from the city as possible. Large parks like Algonquin will be easier for you to open communication with Coral without showing up on Sindrell's radar. Using your powers when you're this emotional in large cities that need a lot of electricity to power them sends off a frequency to her, acting as a beacon. You need to control your emotions and suppress your powers so we can escape."

Dad snorted. "Look around you, we'd be lucky to find a car that isn't smashed! There's no possible way we can quickly get out of the city. Wherever we go will have to be by foot."

"Then we need to get underground. I know a place, it's about an hour walk, but it's in a park. There's an underground tunnel there. That will have to do for now." Zander turned to me. "It will be safe."

Dad sighed. "Lead us."

Zander wasted no time. But as he began to walk past my parents, Dad grabbed his arm, his sharp claws digging into Zander's skin hard enough to draw blood. His yellow eyes set on Zander with a darkness that frightened me, followed by a low, predatory growl. "I've seen what you're capable of, Red. Hurt my family and I promise I in return will show you *my* full capabilities."

Zander nodded as Dad slowly released his arm and turned to me. The glow in his eyes faded back to normal as he held one hand out to me. "C'mon, sweetie."

I quickly ran into Dad's arms. Once cocooned in his embrace, the tears began to flow. He squeezed me in tighter. "I'm sorry I wasn't the one to tell you, sweetie."

I looked into his tender eyes, then to Mom, who continued to glare angrily at me. Her face softened for a moment as she lightly stroked my cheek, but reverted back into stone as she followed Zander around the bend. I knew I had hurt her with this, I could feel her resentment coursing through me. Would she ever forgive me? I followed closely behind as Dad took my hand and led me back into the backyard. My eyes widened in disbelief at the sight before me.

Many of the guests had fled, but a few neighbours lingered amongst the rubble of what was once my beautifully decorated backyard, trying to call their families. Broken trees and pieces of the fence were scattered everywhere. Shattered glass covered the ground splattered on top of fragmented and cracked interlock. The gift table was split in two with all the gifts lying like a pile of garbage in between the broken pieces. The houses surrounding us stood with smashed windows, and caved in roofs. The sound of fire trucks and ambulances sounded in the background.

As I watched, Mom and Zander make their way inside. One thought came into mind, striking a fear in me that instantly made me feel sick. I squeezed Dad's hand.

"Julie! Where is she?"

He quickly drew me in closer, calming my rising hysteria by gently rubbing my arm. "She's fine, she's with Tom."

I frantically scanned for her, letting out a sigh of relief when I spotted her beside our neighbour, Tom. As her eyes found mine we sprinted towards each other, slamming into one another in a tight embrace.

Julie was hysterical. "Thank God you're OK! When I couldn't see you, I thought –"

"I know, it's OK, I'm fine." I tried my best to smile reassuringly until I spotted the gash on her arm. "Jewls, you're hurt!"

She frowned, glancing down at her arm, trying to cover the wound with her hand. "When everyone started running they seemed to have forgotten their manners. Pushed me right onto broken glass. I'm fine, don't worry."

I blinked back tears as I watched the blood seep through her fingers. She was cut deep. I quickly ripped off a hanging piece of tablecloth from the table behind us and began wrapping it around her arm. I cleared my throat. "This will have to do for now." I continued to wrap, feeling the tears slide down my cheeks.

Dad came over with Tom. "Julie, listen to me sweetie, I need you to go with Tom, he's taking a group to the hospital. His wife is on the way."

Tears began to well up in Julie's eyes. She tightly grabbed onto my hand. "No. I'm staying with you guys! I'm fine!"

Dad looked at her with an agonized expression. Speaking softly and slowly, "You're not OK, sweetie. That wound needs to be stitched up before it gets infected. They're going to make sure you get taken care of and get you in touch with your parents."

Tom came up beside us, gently placing his hand on Julie's shoulder. "My wife is an EMT, she was answering a call a couple blocks over when the quake started. She's OK, she's going to take those in need of immediate attention to the hospital. You're losing too much blood sweetheart."

Julie and I glanced at her arm. The cloth had practically already soaked through. She looked at me with glossy eyes, then to our surroundings. "I'm scared."

I hugged her tightly. "Me too Jewls. Everything is going to be OK, though."

Dad chimed in. "You'll be in good hands, Julie. We have to get Zander home. I'll make sure we get to a phone when we can to check up on you, OK?"

She nodded her head, tears beginning to stream down her face. My heart shattered, leaving what felt like a gaping hole in my chest as Dad gently took my hand and led me back into the house, away from Julie.

Zander stood waiting at the front door as Mom threw down three large backpacks from upstairs. The staircase was heavily damaged, but I watched in awe as she jumped, landing gracefully on her feet.

"I knew we'd have to run someday. Here, put these on, it should be enough to get us by for a few weeks." Her voice was flat and bitter. She barely looked at me.

Once we all had on a backpack, we headed out. The street was pitch black with all the streetlights blown out, but we managed to see clearly with our heightened vision. Our car sat flattened under a large branch and pieces of brick. The road was cracked and full of debris.

As we began to walk, an eerie chill set in being surrounded by so much destruction. This was all my fault. I was naïve to think that Zander could come to my party with no problems. I should have told him it wasn't a good idea from the get go, instead of being so selfish. None of this would have happened. My stomach was in knots. My feet felt heavy as I continued to walk, carrying my burdens with me. I let the warm tears fall down my face as I continued to walk in silence.

We took side and back roads. Every now and then we'd see other people walking with flashlights and pictures in their hands, asking us if we'd seen their loved ones. The hole in my chest just kept growing as my guilt continued to spread. Small tremors continued to threaten us. We knew it was Sindrell trying to break through. Dad noticed me trailing behind and slowed down to walk beside me. He nudged my shoulder with his and I tried my best to smile, managing a slight grin. He exhaled, keeping his gaze forward.

"I should've told you about us that night on the porch. Something in me knew better than to think you'd just let it go. I thought at the time that I was doing the right thing."

I looked over at him, eyes wide. Was he blaming himself for my mistake? "Dad, no, I –"

He cut me off, keeping his gaze locked in front of him. "Just hear me out, sweetie. When Coral told us there had been a breach, we knew that if trouble was near we would regain some of our powers and be able to take care of the situation. It was in our ignorance to think we didn't have to involve you. We figured we would experience our powers, not you. You must've been so scared when your powers kicked in." His voice cracked. "It's our duty as parents to protect you. Instead by keeping this from you, we led you right into the arms of our enemy. I'm so sorry we failed you, sweetie."

I couldn't listen to this anymore. "None of this is your fault!" I hadn't realized I was screaming. Mom and Zander stopped walking ahead to turn back to me. I threw off the backpack, desperate to break free from its weight on top of the weight of my actions. "Everything that happened tonight was because of me! Do I wish that you both would have told me what I was instead of me thinking I was losing my mind? Yes, but I made the choice not to tell you what was happening to me! I made the choice to learn more from Zander, encouraging him to try the spell tonight. These were all my choices!"

I began to tremble as I felt a tingle race over my skin with a low static. I looked down at my hands, watching my fingernails grow longer into sharp black claws.

Zander's face wrinkled with worry. "Breathe through it, Princess, you have to calm down."

Mom dropped her backpack with force and stormed over to Zander, her face stone cold. "You think you're her personal coach now? You've clouded her mind with your tricks and charm, but I know better! I know who you really are, Red."

"Mom, stop." I tried to keep my voice stern, breathing through the currents that were now erupting on my skin to try and regain control.

But my plea didn't phase her. She continued on as if she hadn't heard me. "I saw the thirst in your eyes when you came looking for her that night with the rest of the Dark Seekers. The unadulterated lust for bloodshed. *You* had to be the one to take her away from us and watch her die. She was an *infant*! You didn't care then, and I refuse to believe you care now."

Zander looked at Mom with a hard stare. "I cannot change what I've done in my past. Only the present and the future will reveal to you where my heart truly lies."

She laughed almost hysterically. "Your *heart*? You are a creature of the night, a murderer and a soulless monster! You have no heart."

My body jerked and quivered as I felt a scream tear through my throat. "I SAID *STOP IT!*"

My body felt like it was detonating from the inside. I dropped to my knees, holding myself up with my hands in a tabletop position.

"Angel, *no!*"

Zander's scream was the last thing I heard before the ringing started in my ears. There was a fire spreading inside of me. I felt my back arching and contorting. My hands dug into the ground for stability. It felt as if every bone in my body was dislocating itself, popping and crunching more as I continued to rock with tremors. The scorching heat brewing inside me was getting stronger. I had lost all control to its blistering embrace. I could now only surrender to it. I faintly heard words in the background, but couldn't make anything out. Finally, a soothing coolness began, slowly dousing the heat from inside me. Bit by bit, I regained control of my arms and legs, managing to finally stop the tremors so that I could breathe and calm down. Once my body temperature levelled out, I slowly opened my eyes. Zander was kneeling down in front of me, both hands cupping my face, soothing me with his cool touch. His voice was soft, and calm.

"That's it. You got this. Almost there. Just keep breathing."

I exhaled, closing my eyes again, letting his voice guide me back to normality. When I reopened my eyes, I stared into Zander's. His lips curved up in a slight smile as he took his hands from my face to gently lift me up. I clung to him for balance, still feeling a little dizzy. Dad was instantly by my side, looking at Zander with gratitude.

"Thank you," he nodded as he held his arms out to take me into his embrace.

Mom stood flabbergasted, looking at Zander as if she'd seen a ghost.

"It's virtually impossible to stop a transformation once it's been triggered. How did you *do* that?"

Zander kept his eyes on mine. "It's a matter of using the cold chills she gets from me to work *with* her versus against her. Being undead I'm naturally cold to the touch. Your transformation works based on heat. Combining the two slows the process enough for her to regain control."

For a fraction of a second, Mom's face filled with shame. She turned to me. "Are you OK?"

"Yeah," I murmured.

Zander began walking again, this time with more speed. "We have to keep moving, we're about another fifteen minutes out. Once we get underground, we'll –" He stopped abruptly.

In that moment a sharp, icy chill hit me, and judging by the gasps from my parents, they felt it too. They instantly went into a battle stance. Before I could blink, Zander and my parents had formed a barrier around me, looking out into the dark night. I felt the heat radiating off my parents. In unison they both arched their backs, letting out majestic roars into the night. When they stood back upright, they were the most beautiful and terrifying sight I'd ever seen. Their faces now part lion from the nose up, was covered in smooth hair. Their eyes had taken on the full shape and colour of a lion, while the bottom half of their faces down to their abdomen, remained human-like. They had transformed into their full Oleah form, squatting firmly on their thick muscular lion legs, and growling ferociously baring their razor sharp canines at the empty road ahead.

The sound of fluttering grew louder above us as a dark form took shape in the sky, its large wings deafening me with their majestic flapping. With blurring speed, it landed about nine feet in front of us.

There she stood, her massive jet-black wings folding back behind her lizard-like, peacock-coloured skin. She wore a midnight blue, one-shouldered toga that hugged her body like a glove. She was the image of death and absolute beauty with long, wavy black hair blowing behind her. Her emerald green lips pulled up into an evil smile, revealing her sharp fanged teeth. Although her eyes were black orbs of darkness, you could see the excitement in them. She slowly lifted her long clawed index finger up in front of her, moving it side to side.

"Tsk, tsk, tsk. Someone has been a very bad little boy." Her voice was like that of a serpent's hiss.

She raised her right hand, balling it into a fist. I blanched, watching in fright as Zander's body lifted into the air. He screamed in pain as he clenched his hands over the invisible hold she had on his heart.

"Did you think that you were smarter than me, boy? That I wouldn't realize your deception?" She lifted her hand higher, squeezing her fist tighter, which made Zander scream louder.

Fear mixed with fury consumed me. I had to help him, refusing to sit back and watch her torture him. I lunged forward, feeling the heat begin to take over my body.

"STOP IT!" My scream came out unrecognizable and very animalistic.

My parents barricaded me in, Dad speaking in my mind. *Are you trying to get yourself* killed?

Sindrell looked at me, still holding her hand in the air, her face sinister as she began to laugh. If evil had a sound, *that* was it, her icy snake-like voice emphasizing every word. "How *sweet.*"

Zander thrashed in the air, his plea coming out between grunts. "Angel, no!" He tried to reach out to me in warning, but the pain that continued to torment him contorted his hands, bringing them back to hold his chest in agony.

Sindrell's smile widened further as she continued to eye me ravenously. She puckered her lips to me, opened her palm and shut it quickly. The devastating *snap* of Zander's neck rang in my ears. I watched in horror and disbelief as he fell lifeless to the ground.

Sindrell's serpent voice was as cold as ice. "Nobody gets in the way of what's mine."

My eyes fixed on his limp contorted body. A white noise began to spread in my ears. My throat became raw from this sensation that continued to emerge from my mouth; it was then that I realized I was screaming. I couldn't stop. The pain that was shredding my heart in pieces wouldn't let me stop. Tears poured from my eyes as I lunged again for him, fighting desperately against the barricade my parents were holding to keep me in. My body felt like it was on fire again, but this time I focused on it, gave in to it without fighting. I clenched my hands into fists, embracing the burning that made me tremble. A rage started to brew inside me as I locked my glare on Sindrell, whose malicious smile only fuelled the hate inside me. My parents began to quiver in front of me, their voices screaming in my head to stand down.

Sindrell threw her head back with laughter as she mocked me. "What is it with us women? We always go for the wrong men. Don't worry, sweetheart, I'll find you a new toy to play with."

My eyes stayed locked her as the scorching grew into more of an energy, feeding me with its power. It felt like fireworks were going off inside me. I lunged forward again, harshly knocking my parents aside, my vision now red. Instinct seemed to take over then. I lifted my palms up to Sindrell which created a ball of bright yellow and blue fire that continued to grow bigger and bigger. I screamed to release the air inside my lungs, pushing the fire towards Sindrell in one fluid motion.

Upon contact, she flew into the air, landing roughly on her back. She rose quickly to her feet, eyes wild, full of shock and anger as an emerald green glow ignited in her pupils, her lips turning up again in a devious smile.

"That's it, get angry! Show me what you can do. After all, I didn't come all this way for nothing." She brought her palm up to me releasing a force like lightning towards me that made me stumble back.

I stood my ground, hearing the roars of my parents struggling to get back up off the ground. Sindrell was holding them down. There was no time to think, only act. I grounded myself to stand anchored in place, as Sindrell released another blast at me. I held up both palms firmly in front of me as a shield, feeling her power collide against them and bounce back to her, knocking her off her feet yet again.

She recovered again quickly, glaring at me, all humour gone from her vicious face. She slowly wiped the dark blood from the corner of her mouth. "Time to take what's mine."

A fierce wind began to blow as she lifted both hands into the air. There was a burning energy in my palms. I attacked before she could bring her hands back down.

I wasn't me anymore. I was submerged in a force so powerful it kept propelling me towards her. She had no time to recover from each punishing blow of the fireballs. They engulfed her in flames and her serpent-like screams filled the air. It was in that moment that I saw the fear in her eyes. I was stronger than she was, and she knew it. Her magic didn't work on me. It was true. I was indestructible. With my newfound confidence, I lifted my palm in the air with lightning speed and began to squeeze, narrowing my eyes, watching in delight as her body lifted into the air. She clawed at the invisible hold I had around her neck, gasping. She had to pay for what she'd done to my people, my parents and Zander.

Her bulging eyes honed in on Mom and that's when I heard my mother roar out in pain. The sound broke my gaze off of Sindrell to look over at her. She had balled up into a fetal position on the ground, tightly clenching her stomach. That moment of lost focus was all Sindrell needed to break free from my hold. Her majestic wings expanded out from behind her as she began to fly high into the air.

She screamed out, "This isn't over! You *will* be mine, Princess!"

One of her wings appeared to be fractured as she struggled and lifted herself higher and higher into a ball of white light and disappeared. I growled into the air, turning my crimson vision back on Mom, who now appeared to be all right. The force pinning them to the ground had broken and Dad quickly rose to help her stand upright. I ran over, my feet feeling heavy as they pounded the ground. It was only then I realized I too had transformed into an Oleah.

Mom and Dad gawked at me, astounded. Dad pulled me into an embrace, and Mom joined in, weeping.

"You're stronger than we ever thought possible. Your powers are like none I've ever seen before. I'm so sorry we underestimated you, honey."

I was too overwhelmed to speak, as I turned to look at Zander's body. I slowly pulled away from their embrace and walked over, kneeling down beside him. He was still so beautiful as if he were only in a deep slumber.

I heard Dad whisper, "I'm so sorry, honey."

My grief overtook me and I didn't care what it looked like, I leaned down to kiss him softly on the cheek, whispering into his ear, "What am I going to do without you?"

I felt a sob rise in my chest as I embraced his lifeless body.

Mom spoke gently. "We have to get out of here before Sindrell comes back. She might not be alone next time."

I looked up at her, my vision fading from red back to its normal sight. "We can't just leave him here!"

Suddenly, a bright light began to form in front of us, and we all quickly rose to our feet in battle stance growling. A little child-like form with wings appeared, her strawberry blond curls blowing softly behind her. As she spotted us, her face lit up in an angelic smile, her pearl-white wings fluttering in excitement.

"Coral!" Mom yelled out in joy as she and Dad ran over to embrace the little cherub.

My dreams never did her justice. She was truly magnificent to the eyes, such an image of beauty and innocence. Her soft angelic voice was almost musical as she spoke.

"I *beg* your forgiveness! Sindrell locked us out, we couldn't get through the portals. Oh, my king and queen, I've missed you so much!"

Her bright turquoise eyes met mine and she fluttered over to me holding her hands over her heart, her expression full of tenderness and love. She bowed down to me.

"My princess, you've grown into such a beautiful soul. Your powers have surpassed all of our expectations. You are simply perfect."

I tried to smile at her through my tears, but my heart was too heavy. She embraced me, cupping my face with her little hands.

"All is not lost, Princess, you'll see." She softly kissed both my cheeks and flew around to face all of us. "The powers that she possesses are far greater than any in the entire universe. No one except God and the Angels of Heaven have ever struck and wounded Sindrell. You've been given a very unique gift, Princess. You were chosen to bring peace back to the galaxies. Sindrell knows that she is no match against you. However, she is ruthless and won't rest until she can have that power. There's a cave I will take you all buried deep in the depths of the earth. She won't be able to feel your energy and locate you there. We'll be able to regain full access to Uforika and devise a plan of action. Sindrell would be a fool to come back alone. She will be bringing an army. We have to be ready for war."

Her words sunk in. "War? What happens to everyone on Earth? We can't just have innocent people to die!"

A low raspy voice chimed in. "The princess is right."

My heart hit the floor. Hearing Zander's voice sent a wave of goose bumps over my entire body. I looked over to him in complete shock, and before I knew it, I was running to him, flinging my arms around him.

"You're alive! *How*?" A sob caught me before I could finish.

Zander hugged me fiercely, running his hands over my head to soothe me. "I'm OK."

I quickly looked to Mom and Dad for answers, but judging by the shock on their faces they too were surprised to see him alive.

Coral smiled. "As an Obiri, he cannot be killed unless his heart is penetrated, he's set on fire or … decapitation. Anything else will just knock him out for a while." She floated over to him, beaming. "You were willing to sacrifice yourself for the princess and because of that, we are willing to overlook your past transgressions. We see now that your intentions are pure. The Oleah's of Uforika are willing to forgive you."

He nodded his head with a wince, bringing his hands up to rub his neck. "Still hurts."

I couldn't help but laugh through the tears. I reached up and kissed him.

Mom reacted immediately.

"Angel Julia-Marie Seriki!" She marched over to us in a huff. "For the simple fact that we all thought he was dead, I'll let that one slide."

Dad walked up to Mom, pulling her back by the waist into an embrace, smiling at Zander. "You've proven yourself to be worthy of my daughter. You have my blessing. I'll work on getting hers."

Coral cleared her throat. "I hate to go back to the dark and dreary, but we really must act quickly."

Zander rubbed his neck some more. "What Angel was saying is true, if Sindrell comes back here, thousands of lives will be lost. There must be somewhere else we can go that's remote enough that your soldiers can still get to quickly if need be. As long as Sindrell has access to Earth, she will close all portals. Her pride has been wounded, she won't get over that easily. She'll do whatever it takes to win." He looked to me with empathy in his eyes, gently squeezing my hand. My Oleah form didn't seem to bother him one bit.

Mom chimed in. "If memory serves me correctly, there's a planet we used to go to for battle training. Is that still around, Coral?"

"Planet Vox, yes it is! I believe the inhabitants were evacuated when Sindrell's raids began. I'll look into regaining access. We shut down the portal to that planet years ago. Once we reach the cave, I'll set everything up. It's best we get going."

A sinking feeling started to spread in my chest. "So that's it? We just pack up and leave Earth? We have a *life* here! What about school? And Julie?

We can't just leave and never come back!" Listening to myself, I knew I sounded like a spoiled brat, but it was true! Earth was my home.

Dad walked over, gently putting his hand on my shoulder. "I know this must be hard for you sweetie. But understand that Earth was never a permanent home. It was supposed to be temporary. *Our* home is Uforika, and that's where we plan on returning to once Sindrell is out of the picture for good."

I felt a lump in my throat. I tried to be more mature about it. My parents had made that sacrifice for me, I had to do this for them. But it hurt.

"With the portals open to Earth you can always come back and visit Julie, honey." Mom assured me.

I nodded back, leaning into Zander as Coral began to lead us forward.

We walked for about ten minutes into an open field. Coral began to form a circle with her hand, as if she wielded a sparkler. A greenish-white portal took shape in front of us and I watched as Mom and Dad easily walked through, disappearing in its light. I hesitated, knowing that once I walk through this portal, my life would forever change. Nothing would ever be as it once was. I was scared. Scared of the unknown and scared of change. Zander must have felt my apprehension. He gently squeezed my hand, looking at me with compassion.

"The first step is always the hardest, isn't it?" He nudged my shoulder and gave me a slight smile.

I nodded, squeezing his hand back in response and let him guide me towards the portal.

A blinding white light engulfed us. For a moment it felt as though we were on a roller coaster, taking the first big drop. My stomach flipped. I held my breath, shutting my eyes tightly as we were pulled in at inhuman speed to our next location. It only lasted a couple of seconds. I opened one eye to look around once I felt grounded again to see my parents back in their human forms, sitting on a large rock next to an underground waterfall. I looked around in awe. It was like something out of the movies. A massive cave in the depths of the Earth, it was like a whole other universe in itself.

I walked over to my parents. "How do I ..." I looked down at my sturdy lion legs and clawed hands, "go back to normal like you guys?"

Mom chuckled to herself. "This *is* your normal, sweetie. It's going to be a bit of an adjustment to remember that. Once we're back on Uforika, this will be our natural state." I looked down at myself and gulped. Mom gently took my hand. "You have to envision what it is you want. Close your eyes and imagine yourself looking into a mirror as a human. Take in your reflection and envision the change. It will start to take effect, but you have to focus."

I closed my eyes and imagined that scenario. I opened my eyes to peek and was quite delighted at the sight of my human hands once again. How could I ever get used to seeing myself as an Oleah permanently? I wasn't ready to deal with that thought just yet, so I banished it from my head.

"She's a fast learner." Zander came up beside me.

Dad looked at me fondly. "She is."

I took in our surroundings once more, then turned to Coral. "So, now what?"

"I have to return to Uforika to update everyone on what's happening. I should be back here within the hour with our best soldiers to set up camp here until we're ready to set up on Planet Vox." She smiled excitedly at me. "Kovu will be so happy to see you, Princess!"

I awkwardly smiled back at her as if I should know who she was referring to. She fluttered over to quickly kiss me on the cheek before she formed a portal and left.

I looked over to Mom and Dad. "Kovu?"

Dad smiled. "He was our most trusted soldier back home. He loved you very much. That necklace we gave you tonight was his. Before we left he put it on you for strength. You two were very close once, as you also were with Coral."

I looked down, feeling nervous and overwhelmed. There was so much I didn't know about Uforika or any of the Oleahs. So many who knew me that I would not even recognize or know.

"Oh crap!" I slapped my hand to my forehead. "I forgot to check in with Julie, I can't just disappear without talking to her!"

"Angel," Dad began.

I felt my hysteria rising. "I have to know she's OK! She has to know *I'm* OK!"

"Angel, sweetie," Mom tried again, a little louder.

"She's my best friend!" I began to pace back and forth with anxiety. "I can't just toss her to the wayside like spoiled milk. She's going to freak!"

Zander grabbed me with both hands, just under my shoulders to get my attention. "Angel."

"WHAT?"

He nudged his head towards my parents. "Calm down, your parents are trying to tell you something."

I looked to them still in Zander's grip, taken aback.

Mom came over with her cell in her hands. "As Oleahs we have the power to alter the environment around us. So despite us being in a cave, we can generate a current to our phones so that we can still have service." She handed the phone out to me. "Here."

I looked down at the, phone teary-eyed. "So, I can still talk to Julie?" Mom smiled and nodded.

Relief swept over me as I wiped away the tears that trickled down my cheeks. I punched in Julie's number, anxious to hear her voice. It went to her machine. I decided to text her to let her know I was alright and to call me as soon as possible.

I let out an exasperated sigh as I plopped myself down on a large rock near the water. Zander came to sit beside me.

"It's been a rough night, huh?"

I rolled my eyes, shaking my head. "Worst. Birthday. Ever."

"I know it's hard to envision now, but everything will fall into place where it's supposed to." He linked his fingers with mine, giving them a gentle squeeze.

I stared at our linked hands. "I wish you would've told me about your ability to heal before I had to witness you die."

"So you could've been the first to test out the theory?" He smiled light-heartedly.

I kept a straight face, completely unamused.

He squinted his face. "Too soon?"

"Do you have any idea what that *did* to me? I swear I can still hear the sound of your neck breaking and it just makes my gut wrench. She could have killed you."

"But she didn't." His expression became sombre. "It's her way of sending me a message. A warning that I'm easily disposable. She used to seduce me with promises of more power. The thought once enticed me, knowing that I could be next to indestructible beside her as her second in command." He gazed at the far side of the cave. "But then what? What kind of life would I live? The thirst for power is something like an addiction. I would be constantly seeking something more until there would be nothing left. Just darkness. I would never be whole, never truly fulfilled." He returned his attention back to me, his expression hopeful. "But a life with you in it? Now *that* would be worth living."

The warmth in his eyes melted my heart. I caught myself staring, taking him in. My eyes traced over his lips that pulled up in a slight smile with just enough tug to reveal his dimples. When I brought my eyes back up to meet his, his face softened. I brought one hand up to gently rest against his smooth jaw.

"I'll never let her hurt you again." My voice surprised me with its shakiness.

He chuckled, bringing our linked hands to rest against his chest. "Princess, I can look after myself. I knew she would go for me. I let her do it."

"Why would you do that?" I couldn't believe my ears. I tried to draw my hand back, but he tightened his grip, keeping my hand locked against his chest.

"Defending myself would have meant putting you at risk. I had no idea what you were capable of. No one did, including Sindrell. But I did know that with her breaking through, you would regain your full powers, not instantly, but within a few minutes. Letting her take me without fighting back was the only way to keep her focus on me so that your indestructible powers could kick in."

I shook my head, and looked away, frustrated. "She still could have killed you!"

"That was a risk I was willing to take."

I turned back to him, dumbfounded at his confession.

"The things I once had no second thought about, no shame or regard for are inexcusable. If I found you that night in your room fifteen years ago, there's no doubt in my mind that I would have taken you to your demise and felt nothing. The shame and disgust I feel knowing the beautiful soul you've become …" He frowned, looking down at our linked hands, his voice soft. "*Any* risk I'd take for you, no matter the cost, would be worth it."

He brought his gaze up to meet mine again. We just stared at each other with unspoken thoughts and thick emotions. The energy between us crackled against my skin. I found myself instinctively leaning into him, his strong arms shielding me in his embrace as I laid my head against his chest.

My voice was faint. "I don't ever want to lose you again."

He traced his fingers through my hair, resting his cheek on top of my head. "I'm not going anywhere."

I felt the weight of Mom's glares, but I didn't care. I felt safe in his arms as I curled myself in closer, closing my eyes to revel in the moment that I never wanted to end.

Chapter 10: Bait

I opened my eyes groggily. I hadn't realized I had fallen asleep. I scanned my new surroundings, realizing I was no longer with Zander on the rock. Instead I was lying down in what appeared to be a tent on a makeshift mattress made up of material that looked like cotton candy. It was soft to the touch, cocooning me in like a sleeping bag. Zander sat across from me, legs huddled up against his chest, sealed in with his slender but chiselled arms. He sat perfectly still, eyes closed, appearing almost statue like. His face serene, he truly was a vision of perfection.

I slowly sat up, trying my best not to make a sound, stretching out my arms and back. Despite my best efforts, Zander greeted me, eyes still closed.

"Hey," his voice was low and gentle.

"Hey." My voice was hoarse, embarrassing me. I tried to clear my throat. "Sorry, I didn't mean to wake you."

He smiled, slowly opening his eyes. Tints of bright red danced in them. "I wasn't sleeping, just rebooting if you will."

"Rebooting?"

He closed his eyes again, leaning his head back against the tent. "The best way for an Obiri to regain strength after they've been injured, apart from feeding, is to go into a state of rest."

I was fascinated, unthinkingly asking, "When was the last time you fed?"

He opened one eye slightly, raising his eyebrow. "Why do you want to know?"

I felt the heat spread over my face, feeling sheepish for asking such a personal question. "Sorry, it's none of my business."

"No need to apologize, Princess, I'm just curious why you wanted to know." He opened both eyes, his mouth slowly curling into a mischievous grin as the bright red spread in his eyes. "Checking to see if I'm hungry?"

I felt as though my breath was stuck in my throat. Trapped in his stare, a light chill brushed over my skin, not from fear or nervousness, but want. I thought it wasn't possible for him to be any hotter, but with his eyes aglow and that devious look, he was undoubtedly irresistible.

"Are you?" My words were fainter than I expected.

He leered at me, breaking into a low chuckle. "No, and even if I was, you would *not* be on the menu."

I smiled nervously, debating if I should prompt him further. A memory surfaced of the conversation we had in the hallway the day I found out about him.

"You mentioned before that you could paralyze me with a bite. Was that true?"

His smile and eyes faded as his eyebrows tugged down in concern. "I was just saying that to get you to listen, I would never hurt you.

"I know, but is it true?"

He exhaled as if in relief. "Yes. My fangs carry a venom that's poisonous to supernatural creatures. One bite is enough to paralyze our opponents. As you can see, we don't have many shields. We're like humans, fragile. Our speed, strength and fangs are what works to our advantage in battle."

I leaned in, my curiosity at full peak. "So how does it work on humans then?"

"Well," he shifted into a cross-legged position, mirroring me, leaning in as if he was telling old legends to little kids. "Our venom acts a little differently on humans. The initial bite numbs their senses so they feel no pain as we feed. It also allows the wound to close instantly so there would be no trace of foul play." His eyes gleamed as the bright red engulfed them once more. "Our eyes have the power to hypnotize humans so they're more susceptible to our influence. It's the perfect formula to get in and get out without causing a stir."

I smiled, amused. "Fast food, huh?"

He winked. "You got it."

"So, the last time you fed?"

"Quite intent on an answer, I see?"

I smiled apologetically, embarrassed by my eagerness. A light smile lingered on his lips as he hesitated for a moment. "I fed before I came to the party tonight."

He stared expectantly at me, waiting to see my reaction to his honesty. I can't deny that I was a little taken aback, but surprisingly it didn't disturb or bother me. It only enhanced my inquisitiveness. I pursed my lips, narrowing my eyes at him, trying to decipher the politically correct way to ask my next question. I concluded that there was no way around it. I had to just ask him straight, but I was nervous. I didn't want to offend him or make him feel uncomfortable. He seemed to pick up on my vibe, rolling his eyes.

"Come on, just come out with it." He encouraged lightly.

"How, um, often ..." I looked down, twiddling my fingers, "... do you have to feed?"

"If I'm full, I can go three days without feeding. If I haven't had a proper feed, I'll start to get agitated after twenty-four hours."

"Define agitated." I found myself leaning in again, his openness captivating me.

His face remained calm, but his eyes darkened. "The thirst can easily drive one mad. The more the withdrawals set in, the more insatiable it becomes unfortunately. Horror stories have always painted us out as bloodthirsty beasts, but the truth is that, like anything else, if abused the blood can become an addiction. When we drink, it's like a high, a body buzz that brings power with it. Many crave that power and will drain humans one after the other to keep it going as long as they can." He licked his lips. "It's something one has to take their time with. Allowing them to nourish themselves just enough to feel satisfied. Most just take what they need, while a select few abuse it and because of that, we're known as monsters." He shrugged his shoulders, bringing himself to his feet, holding out his hand to me. "C'mon. Best you get up to speed on everything that's happened since you've been asleep. You were out for a while."

I took his hand, allowing him to effortlessly lift me to my feet. I tried my best to smoothen out the wrinkles in my costume and ran my fingers through my now knotted hair to do some damage control.

"How long was I out?"

He lightly tucked a lose strand of frizzy hair behind my ears. "About three hours."

"Damn. I guess the day caught up to me." I smiled timidly, suddenly feeling self-conscious of what I must look like. Clearly his rest had no effect on his appearance. He still looked as fresh as ever.

There was a buzz of chatter that I hadn't noticed before coming from outside the tent. I slowly peeled back the fabric to peek outside. There were now at least a hundred white tents that filled the once open and barren cave. In one corner there was a large group of Oleah soldiers practicing battle formations. My heart rate accelerated so fast it made me feel dizzy. I quickly closed the opening in the fabric tightly with both hands.

"Oh my God." I felt breathless, turning in a panic to Zander. "I can't go out there!"

He smiled, gently taking me by the arm. "You're their princess, they've been waiting a very long time to see you again."

I inhaled, feeling the anxiety spread deeper. "Oh, God!" I sunk down, feeling my knees give way. Zander caught me swiftly with his extra keen reflexes. Supporting me with one hand firmly on my lower back, using his other to tilt my head up to his, his face creased with concern.

"Hey. There's no need to freak. I'll be right here with you." His eyes were soft and encouraging as they searched mine. "Leading is what you were born to do. You can do this, trust me."

I focused on his energy to calm myself down, and slowly nodded to him in agreement. "Everything's just happening so fast. I'm scared." I confessed.

He grabbed both my hands, linking them with his own, as he pressed his forehead against mine. "There's nothing to be afraid of. I'll be beside you every step of the way."

I took in a couple more deep calming breaths, and let Zander lead me outside.

Coral had returned and was speaking with my parents, who had reverted back into their Oleah form. They had both changed into what could only be described as their royal dress. Mom had on the same satin ivory gown and crown from my dreams, and Dad was dressed in a platinum armour breastplate with a thick black leather belt and a short soft leather kilt. His crown was similar to Mom's in the sense that it was a V-shaped band around his head. However, it was pure platinum while Mom's was all diamonds. They truly looked like royalty. I was surprised at how much it suited them.

As we got closer, I found myself walking very closely behind Zander, using him as my shield. When we came up to them, Coral smiled sweetly, fluttering over to greet me with a hug.

"How was your rest, Princess?"

I forced a smile. "Good, thanks." I hugged my arms to banish the goose bumps that prickled my skin as I looked around. I could see the soldiers beginning to notice me, stopping what they were doing to stare. My heart began to beat faster as my nerves started to kick in. "There sure are a lot of Oleahs here."

Coral scanned the room, smiling gleefully. "Only the best soldiers for our princess! Come along, they're all dying to see you."

Before I could respond, she took my hand, giggling carelessly, and began leading me through the tents. I glanced back at Zander with terrified eyes, and he followed behind, taking my hand.

Coral continued to lead us until we came to the circle where all the soldiers were practicing. As we came into view, a hush fell over the cave. All eyes were on me in wonderment. My heart pounded so loud, I was convinced everyone could hear it. My mouth went dry as I stared back at all the yellow eyes before me, squeezing Zander's hand tightly. It seemed to be the only thing keeping me stable. Coral fluttered above us, looking to all the soldiers with a bright smile.

"For years we have been preparing and rebuilding the destruction left behind by the Dark Seekers in hopes that one day our efforts would safely bring our royal family back home to us." She spoke clearly, with confidence and authority. "Everything we've done, every sacrifice we've made has brought us here to this moment. On this day of her birth, our princess has crossed over into adulthood as the most powerful force the galaxies have ever known. It is with great honour that I present to you all our very own Princess Angel."

She fluttered to the side, fully exposing me to the crowd. I gave an involuntary gasp as I stood frozen, immersed in total fear, craving more than anything to run and hide. One by one, each soldier brought their fist to their chest and kneeled where they stood. I tried to catch my breath as my heart rate accelerated. My parents stood at the other side of the cave embracing each other, watching with pride. I looked over to Zander, who nodded encouragingly to me, picking up on my distress.

When the soldiers began to rise Coral continued, "Our princess has been chosen by God to end this war against the sorceress and unite the galaxies. The sorceress has experienced today what it feels like to recoil in fear. It is up to us to stand united behind our princess and bring her down!"

The soldiers lifted their fists in the air, erupting in optimistic cheers. Coral flew down to me, linked her hand with mine, and raised them triumphantly in the air. The roar of the crowd grew louder. I was so overwhelmed by it all. I began to tear up, trying desperately to force a smile as I felt my chin beginning to tremble. They didn't even know me, nor I them, but in that moment I felt deeply connected to them in a way I couldn't quite wrap my head around. The warm feeling that was beginning to blanket itself over me seemed instinctive. I could feel the energy they were exuding, colliding into me with such force, I stumbled. Their hope, joy and trust hit me as if I were feeling it myself.

As the cheers began to subside, the crowd looked at me in anticipation, waiting for me to address them. I opened my mouth, attempting to please them and give them what they wanted, but no sound came out. I didn't have the slightest clue what to say. I stared back, trembling, deafened by the sound of my heart pounding against my chest.

I felt a light tap on my shoulder and turned to face the welcomed interruption. The Oleah soldier before me had very strong features with dark brows, a muscular build like he was taken straight out of a body builder magazine and full lips. His warm eyes greeted me as he quickly brought his fist to his hard ebony chest to bow before me. He smiled sweetly as he held out his hand, signalling his desire to address the crowd.

His voice was soft, but had a deep bass to it. "May I?"

There was something about him that I felt connected to, but couldn't figure out. Trying not to stare, I instantly stepped aside, nodding to him, as I could still not find my voice. He stepped confidently before the herd of soldiers.

"Brothers, I know we are all thrilled to finally greet our estranged princess. However, we must put into perspective that we are new to her, and she has had a very long night. It's best we give her some space so that we do not overwhelm her. We will have an eternity to catch up. Please continue as you were, there is still much we must perfect before we can confront the Dark Seekers."

The soldiers obeyed, turning back towards each other to continue with their training. The unknown soldier turned back to me with a smile. His tender eyes seemed to search mine for a moment before he chuckled to himself.

"Forgive me, Princess. I, too, am still quite captivated with you, it's been so long. You've changed so much." His eyes quickly scanned over me, settling on my necklace. I followed his stare, taking up the necklace in my hands.

I cleared my throat. "My parents gave it to me tonight. They said it was a gift from one of the soldiers."

His returning gaze was so full of warmth I could feel its heat on my skin. "It's a great honour to see you wearing it, Princess."

Comprehension dawned on me. "This is yours?" He nodded proudly. "You're Kovu?"

I couldn't tell if it was tears that glistened in his eyes, or just the way the light caught them. "I am."

"It's nice meeting you … again." I chuckled nervously.

His smile brightened further which made him look younger than he appeared as he brought his fist back up to his heart and bowed his head. When he raised his head again, his eyes met Zander's. His expression became blank for a moment before he forced a smile, acknowledging him with a nod.

"I am grateful for your change of heart, Red. Your knowledge will greatly benefit this battle."

Zander nodded in response. "I will do whatever it takes to help."

Kovu narrowed his eyes, a slight smile lingering on his lips. "If it's alright with the princess, I'd like to take you up on that, Red. You were the second in command to the Dark Seekers. Perhaps you could help with our training?"

I stared stunned at Kovu. "Uh …" The last thing I wanted was to be left alone. I glanced up at Zander, my expression torn. He continued to stare a Kovu with a clenched jaw.

"I trained the Dark Seekers myself, but that was a long time ago. Their fighting style could have changed since then. However, if this is what I can do to help, I will."

He gazed down to me with soft eyes, speaking in my mind. I will have to earn their respect, but it won't come easy. This is a way of showing good faith.

I wanted to tell him not to and stay with me, but I knew he was right. This was just another one of the many adaptations I would have to make.

To the Oleahs, he was last known as their mortal enemy and here I was strolling in with him, shoving it in their faces. I nodded with understanding to Zander before turning once more to address Kovu.

"It's OK with me, but I do have one condition."

"Anything, Princess."

I hesitated for a moment, inhaling sharply and spoke with conviction. "Red is who he used to be. That's not who he is anymore. Please address him as Zander."

Kovu slightly, but sweetly smiled in return. "Very well, Princess. I will advise the other soldiers to do so as well."

Zander brought my hand up to his lips, greeting it with a light kiss. His eyes were soft as they bored into mine with gratitude. "You didn't have to do that."

"Yes. I did." Before I allowed myself to become mesmerized in his stare, I bobbed my head in Kovu's direction. "Go on."

Zander gave my hand another gentle kiss before he let go and made his way over to Kovu.

Kovu nodded his head proudly to me. "You will be a great leader, Princess. I can already tell. Although you don't know your Oleah side, you have the spirit inside you. It's strong." His eyes lit up with his smile as he gave me a final bow and led Zander through the crowd of soldiers.

I hugged myself tightly, attempting to dispel the anxiety I felt without having Zander at my side, watching apprehensively as he addressed the soldiers. I sighed in relief as they willingly obeyed his directions.

I spotted my parents again on the other side and decided to join them to find out where everything stood. Mom greeted me with a hug.

"You did great up there."

I rolled my eyes. "Yeah, sure. You mean, I did great at making myself look stupid up there."

Mom drew back from the hug, holding me back at arm's length. "Sweetie, no one expects you to be anything other than yourself. They're all very proud of you, as are we."

I finally got to take in how majestic Mom looked in her Oleah form. I thought it would be weird to look at her this way, but it felt natural. "Mom, is it possible to feel what other Oleahs are feeling?"

Mom's yellow eyes gleamed with pride. "Yes, we are all connected. When emotions are high our energies bounce off and feed one another." She put her arm around me, guiding me to sit with her on a nearby rock. "It can be absolutely incredible to feed off of the energy of another and have it build you up where you need it most. It's how we stay united and strong in battle, as well as when we hunt."

I glanced back behind us at the sound of swords clanging, taking in another breath of relief to see the soldiers still interacting positively with Zander as he now began to demonstrate several moves. He was fast and fluid in his motions, executing them with deadly precision. Mom's gaze followed mine.

"You know, this isn't easy for me sweetie, to see you with him."

Her voice was gentle, but pained.

I turned back to face her. The hurt in her eyes was evident. "I saw it."

Her face wrinkled in confusion. "Saw what?"

I looked down, ashamed and unwilling to make my confession staring at her face to face. "In the dreams I've been having, I saw when Zander came for me. What he was like back then, how much hate he had." I shook my head in disbelief. "Thinking about it still gives me the chills. I can't even begin to understand how difficult this is for everyone. You have no idea the level of guilt I have about it, but when I'm around him, I can feel the good in him. It's not who he is anymore."

Mom ran her fingers through my hair, letting out an exasperated sigh. "I know." She glanced back over at him, her expression ambivalent. "It almost makes it harder. I hate to admit it, but I too can feel the change in him. I can also feel the strength of your connection to him, and it terrifies me. This test is proving to be my hardest yet."

I didn't know how to respond as I stared back at Mom with mixed emotions. She let out another sigh, turning back to me with a timid smile.

"It's like I blinked and my little cub grew up into this beautiful, strong woman right before me. I guess I just don't want to let you go."

I squeezed her hand gently in reassurance. "I still need you, Mom. Don't ever think I don't. I just ... need him too."

She cupped my face lovingly. "I know, baby." She gazed at me with adoration for a moment, then chuckled to herself. "Enough with the heavy stuff. Come, you must be starving. There are some snacks from Uforika that you have to try! They're delicious!"

On queue, my stomach growled in response at the mention of snacks. I let out a little chuckle as I let Mom lead the way, taking one final glance back at Zander.

Mom motioned to Dad to come along. He lightly jogged over, placing his strong Oleah arms over my shoulder. It was then that I noticed his cell tucked into the front pocket his soft leather kilt.

"Did Jewls call back, Dad?"

"Hmmm. I haven't heard the phone ring, but let's check." He fluidly took the phone out of his pocket without breaking his stride, bringing it up to his face. "Nope. No missed calls."

I felt the unease spread in my stomach as I stretched my neck to get a better view of his screen. "There's still service right?"

"From what I can see, yes." Dad rubbed my arm as he tried to reassure me. "It was chaos up there, sweetie, she'll call when she can. For all you know, where she is may not have any service."

"Yeah, I guess." I bit down on my nails nervously. "I'm gonna call her again, maybe she just had her ringer on silent."

Dad passed me the phone. I paused where I stood, quickly punching in Julie's number. As the phone began to ring I felt a pinch of relief, wanting more than anything to hear Julie's voice. I tapped my foot impatiently as it kept ringing. Finally, after what seemed like an eternity, the call was answered.

"Hello?"

In that moment Julie's voice was the sweetest sound to me, and I sighed, deflating in relief.

"Oh thank God, Jewls! You had me so worried! Is everything OK?"

Mom and Dad looked to me, smiling gratefully as the worry that I hadn't noticed before on their faces dissipated.

She chuckled lightly. "I'm fine, why wouldn't I be?"

I placed my hand over my heart, letting out another sigh of relief. "When I didn't hear from you, I started going a little mental."

Her perky laugh instantly brought a smile to my face. "Oh, Angel, always such a spaz. There's nothing for you to get so worked up over. I mean, you only left me out in the open as a free target for anyone or anything for that matter to claim. Disregarded and unprotected." All humor left her voice as it went flat.

Her words sliced into me with a jagged edge that I was not prepared for.

"What? Jewls." My voice cracked. "You know that's not true."

She snorted harshly. "Oh please! All you care about is that stupid, traitorous new boy toy of yours!" Her familiar voice transformed as she was speaking and began to take on a serpent-like tone. "Poor Julie didn't even see it coming! Quite sloppy of you, Princess, if I do say so myself." Sindrell's serpent-like hisses scorched my ears like acid.

Horror took hold of me. My knees began to wobble as I clutched the phone so tightly, I began to hear it crack. My heart sunk deep in my stomach and I couldn't breathe. I began panting, desperate to get air as I managed to whisper,

"What have you done?"

Her malicious, deadly laugh echoed in my head, making me wince with the pounding it started in my temples.

"It's called taking control of the situation." She laughed again, provoking me further. "You should've seen the look on her face, it was *priceless*!"

A fury grew inside me as her laughter continued to pound against my head. Specks of red began to appear in my vision as I felt the scream rising in my throat, escaping as a vicious, thunderous growl that shook the whole cave.

"WHERE IS SHE?"

Enraged, I began to tremble. With blurring speed Zander, my parents, Coral and Kovu circled around me, their faces serious and concerned. Sindrell's sickening laughter stopped abruptly.

"Careful with that tone when you're speaking to me, Princess," she hissed icily. "Every chain has a weak link. If you ever want to see your precious friend again, you will surrender yourself to me. If you refuse, I will turn her into a creature of the night and you'll be forced to kill her yourself with the havoc she'll unleash on the human population. After I torture her for hours, of course." She snickered. "The choice is yours. Oh, and just in case you think I've killed her …"

I inhaled sharply as Julie's terrified screams sounded on the other end, piercing my heart as she pleaded desperately with them to let her go.

"You have until sunrise to call me back with your answer." She giggled in Julie's voice. "Bye honey!"

When the line went dead, the agony that gripped me caused my knees to give way. Zander caught me, taking me into his arms. I stared at him, stunned, then to everyone that circled around me. I could feel the panic rising in the air as more soldiers began to crowd around.

Everyone's distressed expressions became blurry as the tears began to flow from my eyes. Mom gripped me by the shoulders as the sobs began to take hold of me, tilting my head up to meet her worry-filled eyes.

"What is it? Oh, God, Angel, what's happened?"

I tried to speak through the sobs as best as I could.

"Julie! Sindrell has Julie!"

In that moment, everything seemed to be happening in slow motion. I watched Mom look to Dad, eyes wide with terror. Coral began instantly yelling directions to Kovu to rally the soldiers for battle, and Zander continued to hold me tightly, a low growl rumbling in his chest.

The air became too thick to breathe, and dark specks began to form in my vision as memories of Julie and I over the years spilled into my mind.

The first time we met, she sat beside me in kindergarten, instantly holding up her identical Strawberry Shortcake lunchbox with wide eyes and declared us best friends. We'd been through everything together. It didn't make sense how any of this could have happened. The room began to spin as more dark specks began to blind me. I felt nauseous, craving more than anything for a fresh breath of air.

Zander's voice was almost like an echo in the background. "We're not going to take the bait Angel, but we'll get her back. Stay with me."

I tried to focus my eyes on him, but everything was too blurry. I closed them, desperate for the dizziness to go away.

"We'll get her back Angel, I promise you we will get her back. Stay with me."

Zander's anguished promise were the last words I heard before the darkness took me under.

Michelle Johnson

Throughout my childhood I was always told I had a very creative imagination. I was drawn to stories of mythical creatures and all things that would usually give my peers the heebie geebies. Shows like Tales from the Crypt Keeper and Buffy the Vampire Slayer were among some of my favourites.

I developed a strong passion for design and illustration, drawing the ideas that arose in my head and finding great excitement in bringing them to life.

This led me to pursue a career in graphic design and marketing so that I could always use my creativity to the fullest.

I have always loved reading and the way a compelling story would allow my mind to absorb its detailed imagery. I began to use writing as a tool to bring my creative thoughts to fruition one day, which has brought me to this moment.

I'm a romantic at heart and a sucker for stories about true love which is reflected in my writing and helped bring the Oleah Chronicles to life. I hope you enjoy my first book and through it you experience the eccentric vision that began in my mind so long ago.